BELLADONNA

A CLANCY MYSTERY

JOHN BAYLEY

BLACK ROSE
writing™

Nancy,
all the best!
John 5-2-2015

First printing

This is a work of fiction. Names, characters, businesses, places, events and incidents are either the products of the author's imagination or used in a fictitious manner. Any resemblance to actual persons, living or dead, or actual events is purely coincidental.

ISBN: 978-1-61296-468-3

PUBLISHED BY BLACK ROSE WRITING

www.blackrosewriting.com

Printed in the United States of America

Suggested retail price $15.95

Belladonna is printed in Cambria

In loving memory of my dad, I miss you every day.

BELLADONNA

CONTENTS

Chapter One

Bad News

"Good morning Gil, do you have a minute?"

I was instantly uneasy. Had I become so engrossed in my work that I missed the rapid and often loud footfalls that signaled well in advance, the approach of my boss; a man who never moved about the tiled hallways of his school in stealth? Concerned that I was losing my edge, I glanced down past his crisp white shirt, colorful paisley tie, and perfectly tailored suit, wondering if he'd traded in his brilliantly polished Johnston Murphy shoes for a pair of slippers. The black, mirror-like leather surface, with their perfect tassels peeking out from his pant cuffs confirmed that he hadn't. Somewhat embarrassed, I lifted my gaze and met the inquiring eye of Principal James White, who now leaned casually against the door jamb of my office.

"Good morning Principal White and to what do I owe this honor?" Even as I said it, I knew something was wrong. An unannounced, early morning visit by Principal White usually meant trouble.

"Did you read the newspaper this morning?" he asked.

"No," I said shaking my head, "traffic was bad last night, and I got home much later than I planned from the family fishing trip. I woke up late and forgot to get it out of the box. What did I miss?" I asked, taking my glasses off and laying them carefully on the desk.

"Here, I'll let you read it yourself."

From the leather bound Franklin Planner that had become a part of his being, Principal White produced a neatly folded section of the Oakland Press, which he placed on the desk in front of me. A tiny bold lettered article was circled in blue ink. My heart sank as I read it.

Death in the Village of Milford

The Milford Police reported on Sunday morning that a silver Chevrolet Cobalt driven by a seventeen year old girl, struck three parked cars before coming to rest against the base of a lamp post. The girl, a senior at Milford High School, was pronounced dead at the scene. The girl's family has asked that her identity be withheld.

I looked into the now serious face of my friend and the leader of the school. While Jim White is a great educator, and a brilliant administrator, he is also a man of action. I knew there wouldn't be a lot of discussion on this bit of very bad news. Anticipating my next question, he held up his index finger, rose from his seat, and closed the door to my office before he spoke.

"The girl's name is Caitlin O'Brien. I don't know if you remember her, she came through here about four years ago. It was recently announced to the district leadership that she'd been selected as a finalist to win the School's Scholarship for Leadership and Academic Excellence."

I did remember her, Caitlin and I had met a few times, she'd had a bit of trouble adjusting to the schedule and demands of

Middle School. Over the years I'd recognized her achievements and was pleased that things had worked out so well for her. Caitlin's death was a hard blow to us all; we'd lost far too many kids over the years.

"Yes, I do remember her," I said to Principal White, who now sat on the couch in my office, his right leg crossed over his left, the sharp crease on his pants breaking at the perfect point, allowing the cuff of his slacks to fold over neatly. He had a very familiar look on his face, a look that suggested I was about to get a new assignment.

"Rumor has it that her death may not have been from natural causes, some of my friends suspect foul play," he said.

I have often wondered who these "friends" might be, and how they seemed to know so much, so fast. Given that no more than twenty-four hours had passed since Caitlin's death, and a suspect had yet to be apprehended, the identity of Principal White's very informative friends would have to wait for some other time.

"Gil, you know that we cannot allow this to happen to one of our kids," Principal White said as he stood, and straightened his expensive pinstriped suit coat.

Here it comes, I thought to myself.

"Gilbert, I would like you to look into this."

I pointed to the stack of files on my desk. Each represented a student with a real problem, who needed to meet with me.

"Don't worry about that," he said with a superfluous wave of his hand, "Phyllis has already rescheduled them." Then without another word, Principal James White opened the door to my office and was gone.

I leaned back in my chair, clasped my hands behind my head, and considered what had just been said. A moment later Phyllis Smith, our Department Administration Manager stepped through the door of my office, raised her eyebrows, and took the stack of files from my desk.

"You knew about this?" I asked

"I knew about this last night, when I heard on the news that a teenager died in the village," she said over her shoulder as she left the office.

I watched her go. Phyllis Smith was the very best thing to happen to our lowly, disorganized department. She removed the chaos and confusion, replacing it with clockwork precision. Every counselor was prepared for their appointments, and every student was on time. She brought out the best of us "Freud heads" and ensured that every student received the very best service.

Reader, before I go on please allow me to formally introduce myself. My name is Gilbert John Clancy, and I am by occupation, a Student Guidance Counselor and Academic Advisor at Margaret E. Muir Middle School. I live in the Village of Milford and have been happily married to Sylvia Elizabeth Clancy for longer than I can remember. We have two beautiful daughters; Julia, who is now attending Eastern Michigan University, and Morgan, a senior at Milford High School.

With the help of my brilliant wife, and a select group of friends, I've managed over the years to solve a number of very unique mysteries. This success has cast me into the precarious role of amateur detective.

"Look into this," when spoken by Principal White usually means clean up the mess and make sure the perpetrator is brought to justice; a task which is usually done covertly, and well below the legal radar. With those formalities out of the way, we can now proceed.

As Phyllis distributed my real work to my already overburdened colleagues, I pulled a yellow legal pad from my desk, and began to consider the task that lay before me. Why would someone want to kill a seventeen year old girl? In fact why would anyone want to kill another human being? My good friend Spenser, the detective extraordinaire, made famous by the great Robert Parker would tell you that there are only two motives for murder: love and money, and all things related.

My first stop will be coffee with Sylvia at her bookstore in the village. The Who Done It Bookstore, as the name suggests, specializes in mysteries. On top of being a great wife and mother, Sylvia has run a successful business for many years, and has recently become a published author. After coffee with my wife, I'll call upon Robert Thomas, an old friend and Detective with the Milford Police. After that, I'll begin turning over stones and stirring things up, and see what happens.

The bell above the heavy wooden and windowed door announced my arrival. Sylvia looked up from her work and smiled. Her cat eye glasses, which normally hang about her neck on a golden chain, were perched on the end of her nose.

"Skipping school today?" she asked in the Scottish brogue that always made my heart flutter. Then she rose from her seat, came around the counter, and gave me a kiss that suggested she had really missed me this last weekend.

"Dear, not in your place of business. What will the customers think?" I said.

"Do you see any customers?" she asked, gesturing around the empty store. Then she took my hand and together we walked into her office. She poured us both a cup of coffee and then sat down at her desk. I sat on a couch that had once been in our living room.

"And why are you not at work this morning?" she asked somewhat concerned, since the recent school millage increases had not been very popular with the area's voting constituents.

"I've been asked by the boss to look into something," I answered; sipping an excellent cup of coffee, and wondering why we didn't have this stuff at home. "Did you read the paper this morning? Did you happen to see the article about an accidental death in the village over the weekend?"

"Do you mean the untimely death of Caitlin O'Brien," she answered, her response more a statement of fact than that of a question. How did she already know?

"Yes, Principal White has asked me to look into it and sort things out," I said looking into my wife's beautiful green eyes.

"And where are you going to start?" she asked giving me an inquisitive look.

"Right here, having coffee with my best girl," I said, flirting with the love of my life.

"Don't you mean your only girl?" she answered as the bell over the front door announced the arrival of a customer. Sylvia put down her coffee which would most certainly get cold, and returned to the store's sales floor. I watched how my wife's love for the written word was so easily conveyed in her discussion with a young woman, who appeared to be in her early twenties. She handed Sylvia a list of books she was looking for.

I finished my coffee, washed the cup, and walked past my wife who was talking animatedly about the latest Andrew Greeley Mystery. She found my hand and gave it a reassuring squeeze as I passed, never missing a beat in her conversation. Assured that things were good in my small corner of the world, I now had my own work to do.

Robert 'Bobby' Thomas has been a friend since Elementary School. We have worked together on a number of my "assignments" and our relationship has been fruitful. In return, Sylvia and I have acted as a sounding board and advised him on some of his most baffling cases. If anyone would know the latest about the Caitlin O'Brien case, he would.

The nice thing about Milford is that it is still small enough that you can walk most everywhere you need to go. I soon found myself in front of the Milford Police Station, a small turn of the century brick building with wavy six panel glass windows that pulls at the heart strings of the most nostalgic.

As one of the department's full time detectives, Bobby also has one of the few offices with an actual door. I found it on the building's second floor.

"Good morning," I said to a large head of ruffled brown hair that was focused on his computer screen. When he looked up his eyes took a moment to refocus.

"Gil, get in here man. I figured I'd be seeing you sometime soon." He rose from his chair and rounded his desk to greet me. He extended his hand. I accepted it, and was pulled into the office.

"You got time to see me?" I asked, sitting down on a brown leather couch that I was certain had been in the office since the forties. It was cracked and squeaked like fine old leather should. It was comfortable and it smelled of cheap cigars. Bobby handed me a fresh cup of coffee and then sat down in a chair covered with the same vintage leather.

"You must be here about the death of Caitlin O'Brien?" Bobby asked.

"Yes, our friend has asked me to look into it."

Bobby smiled nodding absently. We had both gone to school with Jim White, whose maturity and leadership early on hinted at the great man he would become. The role of principal came as natural to him as breathing. His passion to help students realize their greatest potential is a trait found in the best educators, but then to protect and care for those kids like they were his own is a quality rarely found in any adult.

"Gil this one doesn't smell right. The Coroner told me that she died of massive organ failure, and he is suggesting poison. It's still unofficial, but if that turns out to be the cause we have a homicide."

His words enraged me. Caitlin Keely O'Brien was a seventeen year old senior in high school with her whole life ahead of her. What could she have possibly done to deserve this?

"Gil, are you still with me?" Bobby's voice brought me back from my thoughts.

"Yes. Sorry, I am just wondering why?"

"That my friend is for us to figure out. The Coroner completed his work in record time. The family, as you can imagine were desperate to get the girl's body back. Mr. O'Brien is an absolute wreck and can barely function. Mrs. O'Brien on the other hand is noticeably upset, but not as distraught as I would be had my only child died," Bobby said suspiciously, sipping his coffee.

"Do you think she had anything to do with it?" I asked.

"Well," Bobby said leaning back in his chair and stretching out his legs, "most children do fall victim to their parents. They may have had an argument, perhaps Caitlin knew some secrets she was going to tell Daddy," Bobby paused for a moment, his eyes unfocused in thought. "Why poison though? How could a parent put their child through such a painful death?" Then he refocused his eyes on me, "To answer your question, they should both be considered suspects."

"What do we do now?" I asked looking into the thick walled bone colored coffee cup that was at least as old as the leather couch I sat on.

"Gil," Bobby said suddenly full of energy. "Right now we need to do what we do best. A young girl is dead, and we need to find out what happened. If it's a murder we need to catch the person who did it." He stood and looked at his watch, which meant our interview was over.

"Thanks for the coffee," I extended my hand and Bobby took it.

"Happy hunting," he said and smiled.

"Same to you," I said turning and leaving his office.

CHAPTER TWO

BENNETT - RICHARDE

I woke early on Tuesday morning and read Caitlin's obituary in the paper. The family would receive guests on Tuesday from 5:00 to 9:00 pm at the Bennett – Richarde Chapel, with the funeral scheduled for 10:00 am at St. Mary's Catholic Church on Wednesday. Caitlin O'Brien died exactly two weeks before her high school graduation. I began to wonder if the timing of her death was a significant part of the motive or just the killer's opportunity. It was however, only the second day of my investigation and that question would join the others on my legal pad.

I arrived early and found the parking lot of the Bennett – Richarde completely full, so I joined the other guests who parked their vehicles along the nearby neighborhood streets. The day was perfect with clear blue skies, mild temperatures for late May, and a light breeze that smelled of blooming lilacs. I fell in step behind a well dressed couple walking quietly, hand in hand along sidewalks shaded by mature maple trees. The simple beauty of the day was an unfair contrast to the tragic death I had come to investigate.

I followed a long line of friends and well wishers into the chapel's largest room, signed the visitor's book, and moved toward the woman whom I knew to be Mrs. O'Brien. As it is usually the case, the immediate family members, now already beyond the shock of the death, must take on the task of comforting those arriving at the service. As the line moved slowly forward, I remembered what Bobby said, and took the opportunity to study Mrs. O'Brien. I was amazed at her composure. Even as her only child lay in a casket surrounded by beautiful flowers in front of the room, she seemed to take great pleasure in being the center of attention.

"Mrs. O'Brien, I'm so very sorry for your loss. My name is Gilbert Clancy and I'm a counselor at Muir Middle School. I knew your daughter very well when she was a student there." Even as I extended my heartfelt condolences to the grieving mother, I could tell she wasn't listening, her eye searching the crowd behind me.

"Mr. Clancy thank you for coming," she said, then smiled sadly and politely pushed me along to greet another visitor.

I followed the line of guests, each of the mourners sharing a brief and personal moment with the deceased. When it was my turn, I was amazed as I looked upon Caitlin O'Brien. Her beauty was angelic; her blond hair was expertly styled, and her makeup artistically applied. There were no visible signs of an illness, or the slightest hint of physical injury that would confirm she had died in a car accident.

Caitlin wore a sapphire dress trimmed with white lace. In her ears were sapphire earrings, and about her neck a diamond and sapphire necklace. In the intimate space that existed between us as I stood over the casket, a beautiful and unique fragrance rose up to greet me. It hadn't come from the dozens of floral arrangements in the room; rather the perfume she wore was distinctive and meant to create a momentary connection, one that would cause you to return to this moment sometime in the future. I smiled because no detail had been forgotten.

As I looked upon Caitlin, I felt a wave of intense anger and then deep sadness roll over me. How would her death affect future events? Would Caitlin have become a world leader, a great humanitarian, or perhaps the scientist who would exterminate the threat of cancer for future generations?

I was drawn from deep thought by the sobbing of a young woman behind me. I turned as a pretty, auburn haired girl stepped forward, her anguish so intense she could barely stand. When her mother met my eye, our grief became one as unchecked tears fell upon her cheeks.

"Why didn't she call me? Why didn't she call for help?" the girl asked sobbing, her eyes red and swollen.

"I don't know honey. I guess we will never know," her mother said trying to console her heartbroken daughter.

I watched the woman pulled the girl close and kiss the top of her head, obviously thankful that she was not the girl in the casket.

I moved forward allowing the family to grieve privately and stopped before the most beautiful bouquet of flowers I've ever seen. My eye fell upon a card, whose conspicuous placement was meant to provide the observer a full uninterrupted view of the floral masterpiece. It said *With Deepest Sympathy, the Bertini Family.*

My friend Salvatore Bertini is a very successful businessman, a pillar of our small community, and one of the finest men I've ever known. I was certain that this bouquet had cost thousands of dollars and was created by the most skilled floral artist in the Detroit metropolitan area. I am also certain that same florist worked around the clock to ensure that this fabulous work of art was the very first to arrive.

Over the years I've acquired some pretty cool surveillance tools. As discretely as I could, I attached one of those technological wonders to the stem of a peach colored rose. The "bug" would allow me to listen to the quiet conversations of the guests as they paid their respects to the victim, and if I deemed it necessary, I could also take a photograph which would be sent electronically to my Smartphone. It is a well known fact that murderers often attend their victim's funeral.

I slipped the Bluetooth receiver into my ear and took my seat just as a group of well dressed, solemn looking girls moved along in the procession. When finally given the opportunity to pay their respects they stopped and looked upon Caitlin, each laid a single rose upon the closed split lid of the casket. I was shocked at how their private words directly contrasted with the façade of their public actions.

"Some are saying that she was murdered," a tall dark haired girl said in a whisper. She looked like she played starting center for the varsity basketball team.

"She probably deserved it," another said, not moving her eyes from Caitlin. "She hurt a lot of people."

"I think she got what she deserved," said a girl with shoulder length honey colored hair. Unlike the others she didn't hide her contempt for Caitlin, nor did she hide the fact that she felt absolutely no remorse, or sense of grief over the girl's untimely death. I tapped a button on the controller in my hand and captured an image of the trio. A buzzing at my side signaled that the image had been received and was now safely stored away.

Next in the procession came a very handsome couple. They were holding hands and the young man was noticeably more upset than his girlfriend. In fact, she seemed angry and somewhat embarrassed by his outpouring of emotion. They stopped and both looked glumly down at Caitlin. Then in a whisper meant only for his ears the young woman launched her attack.

"Why are you so upset? You're not still in love with her are you?"

From my vantage point, I could see the girl dig her nails into the boy's hand.

"No, she was just a friend. I've heard rumors that she was murdered," the boy whispered.

"I don't know why you are so upset after all the trouble she caused us," the bitter young woman said as they moved along to look at the flowers. I pressed the button on the controller and captured the couple's image.

Near the end of the evening a perfectly dressed young man entered the room, signed the guest book, and restored my faith in the nature of human kind. He was greeted openly by Mrs. O'Brien with whom he shared an embrace and a few quiet words. As they spoke she shook her head in great appreciation for his loving words. Then the young man pulled away, kissed Mrs. O'Brien's hand gently and excused himself.

Next he moved to Mr. O'Brien, who'd been in a near catatonic state for most of the evening, still overcome with grief by his daughter's death. Kneeling before the heartbroken father he took O'Brien's hand in his, shared a few private words, and then leaned forward kissing the man's ashen cheek. This fine young man I knew very well, his name is Giovanni Bertini.

He was a perfect gentleman and a tribute to his father. After showing the greatest respect to the grieving parents, he next turned his attention to Caitlin. Giovanni was recognizably different in culture and mannerism from most of the other guests in attendance so when he reached down and took Caitlin's hand it was simply accepted as his way. After whispering an almost inaudible prayer, he crossed himself, then removed a silk handkerchief from an inner pocket of his jacket and wiped away the tears welling in his eyes.

At the end of the evening, just as I prepared to remove the "bug" from its hiding place, a lone girl entered the crowded room. She didn't sign the guest register, nor did she speak to any of the family members. She simply walked up to the casket and looked down on Caitlin. Her dark eyes were cold and her face was absent of emotion. I don't know why but I moved to stand near her.

"Were you a friend of Caitlin's?" I asked searching her face for a reaction.

Responding to my inquiry, she turned and looked directly into my eyes "No, not really. I knew her from Student Council and the National Honor Society." The eyes that looked into mine were cold and grey and lifeless. When she turned to look into the coffin, I suddenly found myself repeatedly pushing the button on the small controller in hand. My senses erupted as they always did when I was close, but would it be this easy? Had I been right and somehow the murderer was standing right next to me? She turned and began to leave.

"Good night," I said. The mysterious girl didn't reply and I watched her walk straight out the door of the chapel.

I removed the eavesdropping device from its hiding place and turned in time to see Mrs. O'Brien and Richard Baker, the Principal of Milford High School walking together. He had an arm across her shoulders and she seemed to be leaning against him for support. Perhaps Mrs. O'Brien's tough emotional façade had finally begun to crumble. After saying goodnight to a few friends, I found them together on a couch, talking quietly.

"Good night Mrs. O'Brien," I said catching her eye.

"Good night and thank you for coming," she replied. Principal Baker looked up as I passed.

"Principal Baker," I said and nodded.

Baker said "good night," in a tone that most executives use when addressing underlings they really don't know. I was certain that Principal Baker and I would soon get to know each other very well.

CHAPTER THREE

THE CAUSE OF DEATH

I left the Bennett - Richarde Chapel with my head spinning around thoughts of the grey eyed girl. Who was she, and what was it that separated her from the many who had spoken ill of Caitlin? I was drawn back from my thoughts when the phone at my side vibrated. The caller ID indicated that it was Robert Thomas.

"Bobby, what do you know?"

"Gil, this thing just keeps getting worse. I just spoke with the Coroner's Office; the girl's official cause of death is cardiac arrest."

"Bobby, she was only seventeen years old. Was there a history of illness, or was she on some type of drug?" I asked, immediately questioning the cause of death.

"No," Bobby answered. The line went quiet for a moment, and I knew he was rechecking his notes. Once satisfied he continued, "Gil she was poisoned. Her heart function failed as the result of a deadly combination of oxalic acid and potassium, which caused the calcium content in her blood to plunge. This led to a lethal heart attack culminating in her death. It appears that she consumed some type of poisonous plant, but the Doc won't know exactly what it was for a few more days."

"Did he venture a guess?" I asked.

"Yes, he said the cause of death would suggest that she died from rhubarb poisoning. I know that sounds crazy, but keep in mind it's his first guess. Gil as you already know, I can buy rhubarb at any grocery store and fifty percent of the people in this village have it growing wild in their backyards."

"That just means that we have to find a person capable of either extracting or obtaining the poison. That same person will have the motive to kill Caitlin," I said in defense of our task, whose complexity had just grown exponentially.

"Gil, there's more."

Bobby's tone suggested that he was about to deliver more bad news.

"The girl was vomiting blood which could have been the product of ulcers in her stomach or esophagus, or the presence of another poison. Whoever did this wanted to make sure Caitlin O'Brien died. The attack was well thought out and she was not meant to survive it."

We both paused for a moment and Bobby finished up the call.

"That's all I know for now, we'll talk soon."

Bobby broke the connection and I drove home thinking about Caitlin and what a seventeen year old girl did to deserve such a cruel and no doubt painful death. Poison, if done right is the perfect weapon. It is not a weapon of rage, nor is it one of impulse. To poison requires planning, and when executed efficiently, requires no physical contact with the victim.

As I turned in the driveway my headlights lit up the front yard, catching a Whitetail Deer and her two fawns cleaning out our birdfeeders. We were lucky enough to find a home on the edge of the country. We enjoyed quite and solitude, while retaining the convenience and community of the village. I noticed that the lights in the house were still on.

When I reached the porch Sylvia opened the door wearing her flannel pajamas. With no makeup and her hair brushed out, she was still the most beautiful woman I'd ever known.

"How did it go?" she asked.

"Well, as you can imagine the death of a popular teenager brought out most of the high school's senior class, their parents, and all of the teachers. I witnessed emotions that crossed the spectrum; from those completely overcome with sorrow, to others who would have spit on the girl if given the chance. I've also been reassured at just how hateful teenage girls can be."

I followed Sylvia into the kitchen. She made us tea and I took refuge in a plate of my favorite cranberry-walnut cookies. My eyes moved from the cookies to a particularly large immovable black mound on the floor. Our dog, that we respectfully call Mr. Jones, is a Labrador Retriever Chow mix who once resided at the Michigan Animal Rescue League. That was of course until his picture appeared in the paper and Sylvia fell in love with the eight-week old fuzz-ball who began his life as Sparkle. Seventy five dollars later, he became a permanent member of the family. That was over ten years ago, and when he is not following Sylvia around the house he partakes in his second favorite activity, which is sleeping.

"Did you see anyone of interest at the funeral home?" Sylvia asked holding a very fine, English Tea Cup in her long tapered fingers. Her fingernails, I noticed were done in a deep red polish.

"Lots, but there was one girl in particular," I said pulling my laptop computer from its bag and the Smartphone from my belt. With the USB cord in place I began to download the digital photos. Sylvia came around the table and watched the images as I indexed through them; each a record of the evening's events. For a long time my wife was silent studying the faces before she spoke.

"You know," she said having now observed most of the visitors, "poison is a very interesting murder weapon. First, you have to understand its effects. If the mixture is too strong and the effects too sudden the murderer could be caught at the scene of the crime, or the victim could be saved. The perfect poison is tasteless in its delivery. The lethal effects come on slowly and so mild at first that they are mistaken for something else; a touch of the flu, sore muscles or a migraine headache, nothing to be alarmed about. This allows the killer to put considerable distance between themselves and their victim. The beauty of a well formulated poison is that the longer the solution is in the body, the deeper the damage, until recovery is all but impossible."

This was Sylvia's gift, she could reason out the puzzle from the smallest scraps of information.

"Keep going," I said, listening closely as she worked out the details in her mind.

"Then there's the poison itself," she said and began her thoughtful pacing of the kitchen.

I was pretty certain that Bobby had called the house and given Sylvia the details before he called me.

"How does one extract poison from the plant? This killer would need some prior knowledge on how to handle the substance, lest the poison themselves. Then of course, when did they have the opportunity to introduce the poison to the victim?" Having finished her summary she smiled and returned to her now cooling cup of tea.

"I certainly didn't see anyone who looked like a chemist or someone capable of the task, unless it was one of the teachers or maybe a student in advanced chemistry," I said typing the information into my investigation notes.

"You know, you scare me sometimes, the way your mind works," I said sipping my own cup of *Sleepytime Tea.* She smiled wickedly at me, rose from her seat, and kissed my cheek before placing her cup in the sink and heading upstairs to bed. Mr. Jones, sensing her departure, followed sleepily behind.

I sat up for sometime with a stack of my daughter's high school yearbooks, looking through the evening's photos and identifying my interview candidates and any potential suspects. What loomed at the forefront of my thoughts was the apparent closeness between Mrs. O'Brien and Principal Baker, which I noted as something to be discussed. With that, I heard the clock ring midnight so I turned off my computer and went to bed.

CHAPTER FOUR

MILFORD HIGH SCHOOL

Wednesday morning began with torrential rain, lightning and deafening claps of thunder. In the parking lot at Milford High School, I watched students run from their cars in futile, almost comical attempts to escape the deluge. Umbrellas were all but useless in the gale force winds. Even the most durable eventually inverted and failed, leaving their owners exposed to the wrath of the storm. I waited in my car until the first bell rang, and then armed with my very best golf umbrella, walked to the school for a meeting with Richard Baker.

I found the hallways of the school full of students finding their way to class, and teachers making last minute preparations. Like most, the school's Main Office was captured in the throes of controlled chaos. I took a seat in a guest chair and quietly watched, waiting for it to subside, I had all day.

"Can I help you?"

When I turned to the sound of her voice I couldn't help but smile. The girl looking back at me was a complex masterpiece of beauty and individuality. Her bright blue eyes had a distant, almost dreamy look. The upturned corners of her mouth suggested that the place she had recently returned from was a very happy one. With her elbow resting on the counter and her chin supported gently in her hand, she seemed oblivious and unaffected by the turmoil that ensued around her. The fingers that cradled her face were elegantly tapered and pale. Her fingernails were professionally manicured and painted with black and red stripes. Her hair was died black, worn shoulder length, and parted in the middle. She wore heavier than required black mascara and eye liner, which further extenuated her pale powdery white skin. She observed me through black horn-rimmed glasses, and in each ear she wore a skull and crossbones earring. She had an enchanting smile.

"Good Morning," I said and rose from my seat to meet her at the counter, "I have an appointment with Principal Baker."

The gothic maiden checked Principal Baker's schedule for the day, "Yes, Mr. Clancy..." She stopped and looked back at me. "Sorry Mr. Clancy, it's been kind of hectic this morning."

I noted that a hint of rouge spread quickly over her pale embarrassed cheeks.

"That's alright Jamie, should I wait here or will you show me in?" She opened the swinging gate at the end of the counter and escorted me to Baker's office.

"I'm surprised you recognized me Mr. Clancy," she said as we passed a number of counseling and administrative offices.

"Jamie, no matter your hairstyle or your make-up you can never hide your pretty blue eyes and your wonderful smile." I was of course lying. Jamie had gone through quite a dramatic transformation since graduating Middle School.

Jamie led me to Baker's office which sat in the executive cul-de-sac. To the right was the office of the Vice Principal and to the left the Dean of Students. In the center of the circular arrangement sat the desk of the Executive Administrative Assistant. Mrs. Busch glanced up at me from an uncluttered highly efficient workstation. In her dark suit, she looked very professional and all business. As we passed I refused to meet her icy stare and knew without a doubt that I had entered hostile territory. We stopped in front of

Baker's open office door and waited. A moment later, the school's principal lifted his eyes and acknowledged our presence.

"Principal Baker, Mr. Clancy is here to see you," Jamie announced, then smiled at me and returned to her post.

"Gilbert Clancy, please come in. Jim White called and said you'd be by this morning."

Baker rose from his desk. He was tall, broad shouldered and handsome. He extended his hand and I took it. His grip was strong and he seemed to draw me in quickly closing the distance between us. As he did his left hand slid up and patted my shoulder; something I wasn't used to on a first meeting. Then again, maybe he remembered me from the funeral home?

"Come into my conference room, I'll get us some coffee."

I followed Baker through his office and into an adjoining conference room. It was much nicer than Jim White's with expensive cherry wood furniture, leather chairs, and top of the line artwork. Baker returned with our coffees and then sat down opposite me at the table.

"How can I help?" Baker asked sincerely.

"I was hoping you could tell me what you know about Caitlin O'Brien. Then I would like your permission to interview some of the students and your staff. I would also like access to Caitlin's locker and her school email account. I'm not sure how long my investigation will take so I will probably be around the school for a few days. I'll be sure to sign in and out as I go." I paused for a moment looking for his reaction. There was none so I continued, "I realize this must sound quite demanding but I find it is better to make my needs clear right away."

"That'll be just fine," Baker said most agreeably, "we have a number of study rooms in the library that should serve your needs as a temporary office. I'll call Mrs. Fortier and let her know to expect you." Baker marked this down on the legal pad he'd brought into the conference room with him. When he finished writing he looked up at me.

"How well did you know Caitlin O'Brien?" I asked and then

watched him closely. I hadn't forgotten his show of support towards Mrs. O'Brien at the funeral home. Principal Baker sat for a moment and looked back at me obviously considering his answer carefully before speaking. I sat quietly and waited for his response. I didn't bring a note pad, nor did I have my recorder. I would instead, listen and watch his words as he spoke them.

"I felt that Caitlin O'Brien was a model student and a great leader. She was President of the Student Council, a member of the National Honor's Society and our Senior Prom Queen."

Baker looked to me, satisfied that he had covered all of her major High School achievements. He hadn't really answered my question at all.

"Is it also true that Ms. O'Brien was a finalist for the School's Scholarship Award?" This time the man's confidence seemed to fail him. Baker smiled uncomfortably and shifted slightly in his seat.

"Yes, as a matter of fact she would have won the scholarship had she not died."

"Prom Queen and Scholarship Winner, that's a lot of recognition. She blossomed into a fine young woman. Did she have trouble with anyone in the school?" I asked leaving the question open ended.

"She did have some trouble in her sophomore year." At this he stopped, rose from his seat and closed the conference room door. "Caitlin was very pretty and very physically mature; she attracted a lot of attention from the male students and unfortunately one teacher." Baker went slightly red in the face and flushed around the collar. It was obvious that he was uncomfortable speaking about a student in such a way. "An incident occurred and she made a formal accusation against one of the teachers. She said he had touched her inappropriately. An internal investigation was conducted, and the O'Brien family was satisfied an apology, and the dismissal of the offending teacher."

"What was the teacher's name?" I asked as Baker took his seat loosening his collar and tie.

"His name was Jonathon Peters. This happened before my time here, Helen Buella was the Principal of the school during the investigation and Peters' subsequent dismissal. I have only a general knowledge of the incident," Baker said.

"How well do you know Mr. and Mrs. O'Brien, are they personal friends of yours?" This question seemed to strike a nerve. I noted a slight change in the muscles of Baker's jaw as he clenched his teeth together for just an instance.

"Pam O'Brien is a very successful Real Estate Agent in the village. She helped me find my home after I took this position and moved my family," Baker explained, confident that his business relationship justified his closeness to Mrs. O'Brien.

"You are new to the area?" I asked.

"Yes, my family and I moved here from Dayton, Ohio."

Satisfied that I had stirred him up enough I stood. "Principal Baker, I want to thank you in advance for your understanding and assistance in my investigation. I will keep you posted on my progress." I offered Baker my hand and he took it. The hand that I shook was now warm and damp. I was certain that the starched white shirt under his very expensive suit was wet with sweat. We exchanged a quick smile and he escorted me from the conference room back into the cul-de-sac.

"Gilbert, Mrs. Busch will give you the location and combination to Caitlin's locker." Baker looked to the sinister one. She nodded to her boss and then turned her icy stare on me.

"Thank you Principal Baker." I looked back to Mrs. Busch and then gave her my very best smile. It had no effect, so I stood quietly and waited. When she was finished she handed me the information on a small piece of paper.

"Wait until the students go home this afternoon or you will raise suspicions. Once that happens, the rumors begin to fly and then the gossip," she shook her head. "The teachers have enough on their plates dealing with these brats." She glared at a young man, who must have been a freshman and in the office for his first offense. He withered like a dying plant and stared at his shoestrings. Then without another word she turned and went back to work.

"Thank you," I said and left the Administrative Offices. In chairs along the wall sat the rule offenders waiting to learn their fate. None but the boldest looked in the direction of the sinister one. "Dead men walking," I thought as I exited the office and reentered the school's main hallway.

CHAPTER FIVE

JONATHON PETERS

The high school had changed dramatically since my graduation. Over the last thirty years it seemed there was an ongoing expansion in order to accommodate the size of an ever growing student body. Those efforts had produced a new library, dozens of new classrooms, a Performing Arts Center, state of the art Computer Lab, and an Engineering Center. The older, once recognizable sections dating from my era had also seen extensive modernization. After spending much more time than I had planned, I finally found Caitlin's locker. Just as Mrs. Busch had predicted there were an awful lot of kids milling around the hallways when they should have been in class, an issue that Principal Baker needed to get under control.

I walked past the locker, noted its location on the school map in my hand and moved on. Curious students, those who should have been in class, stopped their conversations as I passed. Some may have recognized me from the Middle School and others saw me as a stranger. I went in search of the school's library which had moved to the recently completed Northern Annex. There I found Mrs. Fortier at the reference desk.

"Good morning," she said looking up from her work, "you must be Mr. Clancy. Mrs. Busch called and said you'd be along soon. I've set you up in the back study room. It has an internet port, and a phone has been added for your use. If you need anything else my name is Monique." She smiled and offered her hand. I accepted it and looked into eyes that were dark and lifeless; a vivid contrast to her voice, smile, and willingness to please.

"Monique, thank you. I appreciate the trouble that everyone has gone through. This was a last minute assignment given the circumstances and all," I said and released her hand.

"I'm glad I can help. What happened to that girl was unfortunate, and I hope your investigation is successful." With that she turned to assist some students.

On the way back to my temporary office I passed a book case that contained many, if not all of the yearbooks since the school opened in 1869. I removed the yearbooks for 2007, 2008, 2009 and the newest, 2010. It was time to do some research on the students I will be interviewing the tomorrow morning. Also being something of a social scientist, I never passed up an opportunity to study the changing trends.

Caitlin O'Brien became a member of the high school student body with the freshman class of 2006. In that same yearbook I found her as a face in the background of many pictures. She appeared shy and already very pretty. She was a member of the Choir and Drama Club. She appeared in a few Homecoming and Prom pictures with boys who looked to be upper classmen. Nothing unusual about that, pretty girls often date older boys. It is a status thing for both. She hadn't made her ascent to the Student Council, nor had she become a member of the National Honor Society in her freshmen year. She was just another new kid transitioning into high school. From what Baker told me, it was during Caitlin's sophomore year that her life dramatically changed so I reached for the 2008 yearbook.

Mr. Jonathon Peters and Ms. Cynthia Alexander were the two full time faculty members of the school's Art Department at the time. Peters was a nice looking man, casually dressed in a collarless shirt, longish brown hair, and a well-trimmed goatee. He played the part of an artist very well. His smile suggested the carefree and slightly rebellious spirit of one who refused to conform to the expected norm. What really caught my attention was that he looked truly happy with his lot in life, something that has become harder for people to find these days. He certainly did not look like the predator that Baker had described earlier.

I continued to flip through the yearbook finding the photos of friends I haven't seen for a very long time; all are fine educators, and all had become full time faculty members. Linda White, no relation to the much respected leader of our Middle School, was Head of the English Department. Her responsibilities included Yearbook, The Journalism Club, Shakespeare and English Literature Study. Linda's an old friend with a sharp and perceptive eye, and she misses very little. She would be a great source of information about the goings on in the school.

At two o'clock Linda entered my office and flopped down on the small couch that Mrs. Fortier had thoughtfully included in the hastily prepared office.

"And what are you doing here?" she asked allowing her head to fall lazily back on the couch cushion.

My friend looked exhausted. I'd had many days like this myself. The job of an educator, while rewarding is very stressful, and Linda appeared to have a lot on her plate. Among other things, the management and creation of the school's yearbook is a full time job. I'd led that same activity at my own school many times in the past.

"I've been given an assignment to investigate the untimely death of Caitlin O'Brien." Linda did not speak for what seemed like a full minute, lost in thought about what I had just said. "Do you have time to talk?" I asked breaking the silence, "and would you like a cup of coffee?" I was getting VIP treatment. In addition to a private office, Mrs. Fortier had provided me with my own coffee maker and supplies. If this kept up, I might never leave.

"Yes I would thanks," and with a movement that suggested she should also be in charge of the Drama Club, Linda drifted over and took a seat at the table I now called my desk. I poured two cups of coffee, handed one to Linda and took the second for myself. Then violating all rules of propriety and common courtesy, I launched into the issue of Caitlin O'Brien.

"Having been employed at this fine institution of learning for so long, you probably have a pretty good idea of what goes on. This morning I spoke briefly with Principal Baker, who told me that Caitlin O'Brien was the Student Council President, a member of the National Honor Society, and soon to be Prom Queen. And if that were not enough, she would have won the School's Scholarship for good measure. Linda this cannot be the same girl that went through Muir Middle School. In her freshmen and sophomore years she was just another kid in the crowd. How did she suddenly gain all that power and popularity? It doesn't make sense." I stopped rambling only after I ran out of breath.

"Gilbert it is very nice to see you too. How's Sylvia? It's been a while since I've been to the store," Linda said, then smiled and sipped her coffee.

She was taunting me, she would answer my questions when she damned well pleased and not before. I smiled back, acknowledged the error in my ways, and sipped my now cooling cup of coffee.

"Linda, please excuse my violation of common decency. It is good to see you and I appreciate that you have stopped by to visit. I will pass on your greetings to Sylvia, whom I'm sure will call given the fact that it has been far too long since she last saw you. My girls are doing well," I paused for a moment trying to cool my growing impatience at Linda's little game. "May we now return to our discussion?"

"Yes," she said satisfied that we now understood who was really in charge of the interview.

I calmed myself and then continued. "It has been my experience that the type of status and influence that Caitlin achieved is a notable trait throughout a child's life. She did nothing in the middle school, she did nothing in her freshmen and sophomore years, and then she's everything. What do you make of it?" The expression on Linda's face told me that my analysis of the situation was headed in the right direction.

"To answer your first question," Linda began, "Ms. O'Brien's rise to power seems to have been very well orchestrated."

"By whom," I asked.

"I honestly believe that Principal Baker had something to do with it. He seemed to take an immediate interest in a few key students upon his appointment. I'm not sure why, he may have been given some marching orders by the School Board. He immediately began to question the grades we were handing out, and in some cases he changed them before the final submission to the district. I truly believe he put Caitlin and a few other students on the fast track."

Linda's last statement was pretty damning and I noticed that she turned to look for anyone within earshot of the conference room.

"Thank you for sharing that with me." I caught her eye and gave her a look that showed my gratitude. Statements like that would surely end a career if overheard. "One more question if you don't mind."

"Alright," she said and rose from her seat to get another cup of coffee. She motioned to me for another cup and I declined, I'd already had more than my quota for the day.

"Can you tell me something about Jonathon Peters and the issue with Caitlin?" Linda flushed and then became ashen. She pulled the conference room door shut this time and then took her seat.

"One thing you need to know about Caitlin O'Brien is that she was ruthless. I watched how she manipulated her friends. I overheard things in my classes and the clubs. She took what she wanted, when she wanted it, with no remorse or guilt, and never an apology. To be quite honest I think she was a borderline sociopath, but I will leave that to your expert opinion.

It appeared to me that she had always been that way. It was subdued during her freshmen and most of her sophomore year. The incident with poor Jonathon seemed to be the catalyst for her rise to power." Linda stopped, took a Kleenex from the box on the table, and dabbed at the tears welling in her eyes. She took a deep breath, exhaled slowly, and then went on. "It happened in the spring of 2008, when Helen Buella was still the principal of the school. A Michigan State Police Detective, a high ranking official of the School District, and an Attorney representing the O'Brien family showed up at Helen's office. There were rumors that something had happened, but everyone remained tight lipped about it. They told Helen that Jonathon had inappropriately touched Caitlin in the Art Supply Room.

When asked, Jonathon strongly denied the charge, and after a terrible shouting match between Jonathon, the O'Brien's attorney, and the school district representative, he was suspended. At that point Caitlin became the center of attention; she was the victim and a survivor, and her popularity was on the rise. Helen Buella retired shortly after the incident, she believed that Jonathon was innocent and he was fired to save the district's reputation. That's when Baker came to the School."

I noticed that Linda didn't use Baker's professional title. I could tell she disliked him immensely. After a short pause to dab at her eyes she went on. "Jonathon Peters never set foot in the school again and he would never teach again. After such an unfounded allegation he was disgraced personally, socially, and most important professionally. It just wasn't fair." Another tear streamed down her face. "After the inquisition was over they never even brought charges against him. The O'Briens are cruel people who found pleasure in ruining a good man's life. Jonathon's family owned a cottage near Mackinaw City. That's where they found him after he committed suicide." Linda wiped more tears from her eyes as the school bell rang marking the end of the day.

"Thank you, I know that was hard." I stood, came around the desk and offered her my hand. She accepted it and I helped her from her chair.

"Tell Sylvia I'll stop by the store soon, we have some catching up to do," Linda said.

"I will," and with that, Linda White was gone.

In addition to being one of the most dedicated educators I know, Linda is also a great humanitarian. While no names were mentioned, I remembered some of the details of the incident from discussion in our staff meetings. Shortly afterward we were flooded with memos and additional training classes. It was the sort of thing that happened when a major breach occurred in the school district's moral fiber. I never knew his name, nor had I known about the suicide. Before the investigation was over I would know the truth about Peters and if possible, I would clear his name.

At four thirty, Monique Fortier stopped at the conference room door, "Good night Gil."

"Good night and thank you," I said, very appreciative of how well I was being taken care of.

"You are very welcome. The school doors remain open until six o'clock then they lock automatically. Our custodians are not very nice about turning off the alarm and letting people out," Monique warned as she turned to leave.

"Thanks, I'll keep that in mind. I have a bit more work to do before I leave." I watched her disappear into the darkness. A moment later I was alone in the library with more questions than answers and one more task to complete.

CHAPTER SIX

THE SCHOOL LOCKER

At five o'clock I closed and locked the door to my library office and went in search of the day's final task. The school corridors echoed with the many after school activities currently underway. In a large auditorium the school's latest theatrical production of *The Fiddler on the Roof* was rehearsing in preparation for opening night. In full costume, the cast sang and danced about the lighted stage. Further down the hall and with similar fervor, the school's Track Coach was delivering a last minute pep talk, or it might have been a butt chewing. I couldn't tell for sure.

Caitlin's locker sat in a quiet hallway far from the noise. I was thankful that I hadn't passed a teacher, custodian, or student along the way. If things went well I wouldn't be bothered in the execution of my task; a surprised burglar is always a bungler. Before starting I double checked for my Middle School ID, and the note signed by both Principal Baker and Principal White guaranteeing me immunity from prosecution or termination of employment. Satisfied that all was in order I went on.

With Bobby's immense caseload I was certain that his investigation had not yet reached Caitlin's locker. With that in mind

I put on a pair of light weight cotton gloves that I'd extracted from the investigation kit, which occupied one section of my computer bag; lest I mistakenly leave my own fingerprints on a potential crime scene. This was important given the fact that I was about to break the law.

The combination provided by the evil Mrs. Busch was correct and the locker door silently swung open. With a small pen light; another tool used by only the very best detectives and burglars, I began my search of the locker careful not to disrupt the integrity of the evidence.

After working with children for so many years, I have observed that a school locker soon becomes the student's second home. I've walked past some memorable lockers. Some that were full to the coat hooks with dirty clothes, and others that reeked of rotten lunches. One could only guess what their bedrooms at home must have looked like.

To my surprise Ms. O'Brien's locker was relatively neat. I started with the top shelf where she kept her personal things; a bag of make-up, hairbrush, toothbrush and tooth paste, and feminine toiletries. The locker's second shelf which was dedicated to academic material was spartan at best; the Algebra, Physics, and Political Science books looked relatively untouched. This was certainly odd when we consider that she was a noted scholar. I would have expected the books to be jammed into an overloaded backpack or wheeled bag. Also absent were the jump drives, pens, highlighters, and report folders which have become standard equipment for all college bound students considering the amount of research and workload they were expected to maintain.

When the light fell upon a small black leather case, my heart skipped a beat and I knew that I'd hit pay dirt. I opened the case and touched the device's small input pad with the tip of my index finger and the screen energized. I was relieved to find that Caitlin had not secured the device with an ID or password and pulled my sleeping laptop from its bag. I quickly hooked up a USB cord, and with a few quick commands I copied the contents of the tablet into a folder named "Caitlin."

In less than fifteen seconds the download was complete. I removed the USB cord, replaced the tablet, and slid my laptop back into its bag. The locker's remaining contents, or should I say the absence of contents, threw up warning flags right away. Seniors in their last weeks of school are expected to turn in Final Reports. Where were they? Where was the evidence demonstrating that this girl was such a highly recognized student scholar?

My attention was drawn to the bottom of Caitlin's locker which was covered with notes and cards of all sizes, and on all paper mediums; ranging from folded sheets of notebook paper to expensive stationary. From a kneeling position before the locker I glanced up toward the open door which had rectangular ventilation holes that doubled conveniently as mail slots.

I had to laugh at the ingenuity of one of Caitlin's well wishers. To ensure that their correspondence was not overlooked among those now occupying the bottom of the locker, the card, carefully selected to fit exactly through the slotted opening, hung suspended from a string, which was attached to a wad of tape neatly jammed in the ventilation slot. Someone had thought long and hard about that one.

I never open sealed letters or mail, but I could tell by the handwriting on the very nicest cards that they had come from the same admirer. Among the other correspondence that lay at the bottom of the locker I found multiple invitations to the Senior Prom, and just as many invitations to dinner. There were notes from various staff members reminding her that she had missed detention sessions or assignments. Those notes; on the traditional pink format with the strip of adhesive on the back were crinkled up and thrown among the rest occupying the bottom of the locker. A number of the notes to my surprise were from Principal Baker.

Still looking, I found an unsigned note that simply said, "*I saw you cheating in Physics Class and I am reporting it to Mr. Cooper.*" The final note I found was from a girl named Brooke which said, "*I have a date with Luke tonight. Call me tomorrow and I'll give you all the details!!*" Brooke was actually Brooke Kincaid, whom I'd identified as the emotionally devastated girl at the funeral home.

She would be my first interview in the morning. With all the notes and then the lack of academic evidence in her locker, I questioned how Ms. O'Brien had risen to the reported level of academic celebrity.

With the locker now back in the condition from which I'd found it. I closed the door, spun the lock, and removed my gloves. My first foray into the secrets of Caitlin O'Brien's life had taken less than thirty minutes. Heeding Monique's warning I hurried toward the nearest exit. As I reached the end of the hallway I saw the glowing red exit sign pointing to my left. I reached the door moments before the automatic locks engaged. More importantly, Sylvia had texted me several times and I knew that my dinner was getting cold.

CHAPTER SEVEN

TOO MUCH MONEY

The days were getting longer as the year raced toward the Summer Solstice. I phoned Sylvia and told her I would be a bit late, and then asked her to keep my dinner warm a little while longer. Even the most reasonable of women have their limits and I knew that I had reached Sylvia's. There are some things that are sacred and just should not be messed with. For Sylvia, dinner was one those things. In a tone that suggested I would be granted forgiveness only once, she said she would.

"Alright, but don't be long." These words were not followed by her usual and pleasant "goodbye," but by a sudden loss of connection. Did my cell phone just fail? It was highly unlikely. I had yet to find a dead spot in the village after many years of use.

I was headed to Chestnut Hills, a very exclusive subdivision which had been recently developed on the border of Kensington Metro Park. I turned off Milford Road and onto Fairview Drive which wound through the rolling hills of the affluent development. The elegant homes, many with a purchase price in excess of one million dollars, stood regally in the shade of trees.

The land where Chestnut Hills now stands once belonged to Mr.

Ambrosi Pensecroft, an Italian immigrant who came to Milford in the late 1800s. The two hundred acre parcel was tied up for years in probate court with the passing of his only daughter Maria. As soon as the parcel became available, the bidding wars erupted and the remaining relatives of Ambrosi and Maria Pensecroft became very wealthy people. I'd come to the exclusive neighborhood for two reasons. First, to see Caitlin O'Brien's home and understand her lifestyle, and second, to see just how far she'd driven before crashing her car in the village.

Bobby sent a text shortly before I left the school confirming that Caitlin O'Brien died after consuming a cocktail of poisons. The first poison was a derivative from the rhubarb plant. The second poison was Isopropanol, which is commonly found in rubbing alcohol and glass cleaner, which shed a bit more light on the knowledge and background of the killer. Both were very common; our killer had chosen his or her ingredients very well.

After looking upon wealth I would never have and didn't want, I stopped in front of 1567 Oak Lane, the address of record for Caitlin O'Brien. The home sat deep off the road on a multi-acre site. From the road I could see the rolling grounds of perfectly mowed lawn, dotted with manicured flowerbeds. In the distance rose the steep, blue shale tile roof of the French Provincial manor house.

"May I help you?"

I jumped in surprise and turned quickly to the driver's window. I was so caught up in the details of the O'Brien home that I completely missed the approach of a woman in jogging shorts, tee shirt, and walking shoes. Adding more salt to my already wounded ego was the chestnut colored Irish Setter that pulled against her lead and was now barking loudly. I was sure the woman could tell that my Subaru didn't belong in this neighborhood dominated by Mercedes, Jaguars, and BMWs.

"Actually I was going to call upon Mr. and Mrs. O'Brien with my condolences. I am counselor at the Middle School and knew their daughter well." I told the truth figuring I shouldn't push my luck with this suspicious woman.

"I haven't seen them for days. What a tragedy to lose their only daughter," she said stepping closer and leaning toward the car door. I could see that she was giving the interior of my vehicle a quick once over to assess if my story held any appearance of the truth.

"I guess I'll try another day." I said and turned around in the cul-de-sac. I waved to the doubtful woman who did not wave back. Watching me pass I was certain she had committed my license plate to memory. I would probably get a call from Bobby in the morning.

The immensity of the house and richness of the O'Brien's lifestyle immediately raised more questions. A successful Real Estate Agent and Corporate Executive would have to be at the very top of their respective pay scales to afford the mortgage, upkeep, and tremendous financial burden imposed by the village property taxes. The tax payers had contributed a great deal to the renaissance of Milford High School and the large budgets we enjoyed in the school district. Appreciative as I was for that, the O'Brien's presumed wealth did not set well with me. Was something illegal going on? Lots of people are killed when those agreements go bad. What if either or both of Caitlin's parents had crossed a really bad guy who felt that killing the daughter would be a more painful lesson than just murdering the offending adult? The answer to that question, I would know in a few days.

For know I needed to go home and apologize to with my wife, eat dinner, and get to bed early. Tomorrow promised to be a very interesting day.

CHAPTER EIGHT

BROOKE KINCAID

I was up early, dressed, and finished breakfast long before sunrise. My first interview would be with Brooke Kincaid, whom my daughter Morgan informed me was Caitlin O'Brien's best friend. The funeral was over, but not soon forgotten, especially in the minds of the school administrators, who closed the high school for the day, given the number of students and faculty members who chose to attend the service. It was quite a tribute to a girl who seemed extremely popular, yet disliked by so many of the school's general population. With the memorial service behind us, life would quickly return to normal, and I could get back to work.

I was the first to reach the school, except for the unhappy custodian whose morning ritual of coffee, donuts, and the newspaper was interrupted by my request for admission to the library. Now with my own coffee in hand and laptop fired up, I opened the recently copied directory of files from Caitlin's tablet. From a high level, the information was organized into five main folders: Friends, Student Council, National Honor Society, Email, and Texts.

There were thousands of texts so I decided to begin with email.

Her wireless tablet would continue to receive messages as long as the battery remained charged. In the days just before her death Caitlin received dozens of emails from Brooke Kincade, her mother, and other close friends. I noticed that a number of the untitled emails consisted of a single word, a complex formula, or a number. It appeared that Caitlin and many of her co-conspirators had learned to utilize the technology very well. In other words, she had become very skilled in the art of high tech cheating.

I found a number of emails congratulating her on becoming a finalist for the School's Scholarship. The official message came from Mrs. Irene Vincent, Head of the School's National Honor Society Chapter. The message had also gone to a girl named Emmeline Fortier and a boy named James Washington. It seemed odd that this email was sent on the Friday before Caitlin's death, according to Principal Baker she'd already won.

In the quiet of my library office time stood still. The world outside my door however, carried on at its usual hectic pace and soon the library was full of students; some desperate to squeeze in last minute studying for final exams, and those who had either completed their own tests, or had simply given into summer early. I sat for a while and watched Monique Fortier happily carrying out her duties. Her daughter Emmeline, the girl I'd run into at the funeral home was also one of the finalists for the scholarship. For many students it represented the only opportunity they would have to attend an Ivy League university; an opportunity that might motivate one to eliminate the competition. With that happy thought in mind, I moved Emmeline into the number two slot of my interview list.

I continued to search the email and something caught my eye. Again, as I had found in Caitlin's locker, there were a number of messages from Richard Baker. *Please see me at the end of the day. I need to speak with you immediately! Call my office!* It seemed odd that Baker would be sending messages to Caitlin's personal email account. Linda's observation of the situation was absolutely correct.

The evidence so far suggested that Baker had taken a very

special interest in Caitlin O'Brien. Why would he have Caitlin's personal email address, and then send her so many traceable messages? Baker had made a critical error. He should have never allowed himself to get so close to this student, let alone a student in competition for a six figure scholarship, on whose decision board, he was a voting member. I now began to have my own suspicions. Caitlin's death, or perhaps her silencing, would have most certainly saved one's marriage and professional reputation, if immoral or unethical acts had occurred.

At eight forty five Brooke Kincade stood at the door of my office. "Mr. Clancy, you wanted to see me."

I stood as Brooke entered the conference room, "Good Morning and thank you very much for taking time out of your busy day for me." I extended my hand and she accepted it.

"Are you still at the Middle School?" she asked.

"Yes," I said gesturing toward a round table with four chairs that I had planned to use for the interviews. Brooke Kincade had blossomed into a very pretty seventeen year old girl. She had auburn colored hair, perfectly applied makeup, a healthy athletic tan, and the lean figure of a runner. I knew from the yearbook and many newspaper articles that she'd enjoyed stellar success in Cross Country and Track during her career at Milford High School. She wore a short summer skirt, sandals, and a top that revealed just a hint of midriff. She sat in the chair directly opposite of me, leaned back slightly, and crossed her legs.

After many years in the field of education I've learned that when having a discussion with any student the locale should be public enough to permit full view of the exchange, yet private enough for personal conversation. My conference room office afforded me all of those amenities. My experience as a detective also taught me that the eyes tell the story. The nuance of the voice can be deceiving, but the eyes never lie.

"Brooke, I've been asked by the school district to conduct a private investigation into Caitlin's death. I do not represent the police in this matter. I work for James White, the Principal of the Muir Middle School and my findings will be shared with him at my own discretion. You can feel comfortable that anything you say will be kept in the deepest of confidentiality."

"Alright," Brooke said and nodded her head.

"I'm here because Caitlin died of unusual circumstances. If it turns out to be a homicide then we must work quickly to bring the perpetrator to justice. All we're going to do this morning is talk."

"To be honest, I'm surprised that someone didn't go after Caitlin sooner," Brooke began, her voice and emotions a sharp contrast to what I had seen only days before. "I was Caitlin's friend, but I didn't always agree with the way she treated people. She would use people and then just toss them aside. She didn't care who she hurt, and she never felt guilty about the damage she'd done. To her it was just a game, and I was sure it would eventually catch up with her."

When she paused I took the opportunity to ask my first question. "So what I heard you say is that Caitlin intentionally made trouble for other people?"

"Yes, she dated Giovanni Bertini last summer. They met at a party thrown by Caitlin's parents. Giovanni fell head over heels in love with her, and more than once talked about marriage. He showered her with jewelry and gifts, and then he proposed to her. She led him around like a puppy and then dumped him flat. He was devastated and embarrassed."

"Do you think Giovanni hurt Caitlin?" I asked.

"I think he could have. I saw him get mad once and you know who his father is..." She stopped and looked around the library, apparently concerned that someone might overhear, "you know a mobster."

"I don't know Giovanni or the Bertini family that well. I do know that Mr. Bertini is a very successful businessman and a highly respected member of this community. If he is a mobster, I would be very surprised."

Brooke didn't say a thing. Instead she gave me a serious, "I don't think you know what the hell you're talking about" look. I was so used to it from my own two daughters that I blew it off and encouraged her to go on.

"Then there was Tommy Richardson. Caitlin stole Tommy away from his long time girlfriend just before Homecoming last fall. She wanted to date the Homecoming King and once the event was over, so was Tommy. She laughed and nicknamed him "puppet" because he was so easily manipulated. I doubt she ever thought about Tommy's girlfriend Becky. She didn't even go to her Senior Homecoming Dance. She bought a beautiful gown and didn't even go to the dance."

"What is Becky's last name?" I asked.

"Her last name is Smith."

I remembered Tommy and Becky from the funeral home, and how she had verbally attacked his show of emotion toward Caitlin.

Finally, we'd reached the pivotal point in the interview and the moment of truth. "What do you know about Caitlin and Mr. Peters?" After asking the question, I leaned back in my chair and watched the waves of emotion as Brooke chose her response carefully. Her face grew pale, and for a moment I thought I'd gone too far. We both sat quietly for some time before she finally spoke.

"Caitlin told me that Mr. Peters brushed up against her in the art supply room. She thought he was coming on to her. I told her she was mistaken and that Mr. Peters wasn't that kind of a man, but when her mom got wind of it, all hell broke loose."

"Did Caitlin talk much about it?" I asked.

"Not really, I think she enjoyed being the victim. She got a lot of attention and that's when she really began to change."

I nodded my head in understanding, looked at Brooke and encouraged her to go on.

"She continued to tell everyone that there had been real contact, leaving the rest to their imagination. She said he deserved what he got. I thought she was lying and being coached by her mother. Poor Mr. Peters lost his job. I wanted to say something in his defense, but my mom and dad didn't want me to get involved."

Brooke looked away for a moment and then returned to catch my eye. I decided to continue with more of the difficult questions. "What did you think about Caitlin's academic success?"

"I wasn't sure how she did it. We spent a lot of time together. I wasn't getting all of my homework done and I don't know how she did hers. I never remember her ever once saying she couldn't go out because she had too much homework, most of the time she called me. Apparently she did enough to get by. The nerds in the National Honor Society were in an uproar when she was nominated and then became a member. When it looked like she might win the School's Scholarship they swore it was a set-up. I heard that some of the parents had threatened to sue the school district."

I noted that those final words came out of partly smiling lips, a silent celebration of Caitlin's victory.

"Based on what you've told me, can I assume that you and Caitlin were together most of the time?" I asked.

"Yes, we were together all of the time, unless one of us had a date."

"And you were with Caitlin on the night of her death?" Even as I said it, I knew that I had pushed Brooke Kincaid over the line.

"Yes, I was."

Her voice was now cold and defensive. I needed to make a quick recovery. "Brooke, I'm not accusing you of any wrongdoing. I'm just hoping that something you saw, somewhere you went, or someone you talked to that night might give us a clue that will solve the mystery behind Caitlin's death." Brooke seemed to ease with my words.

"Well," she continued, "we went to the school dance on Saturday night. We stayed out really late and I told her I would call on Sunday. She was on her way to my house when she died." The young girl's emotions finally spilled over. I handed her a few tissues from the box on the table, and then laid a fatherly hand on her forearm. A moment later she rose from her seat and I did the same.

"Thank you Brooke and I promise that I'll find out what happened to Caitlin," I said as she turned to leave.

"I know you will," and with those words of confidence Brooke Kincaid left my conference room office. I turned to my desk, opened the computer, and began to type notes from the interview.

Brooke's description of Caitlin was honest and exactly what I would have expected from her best friend. However, I did not like what I heard. Caitlin's actions would certainly suggest the behavior of a sociopath. She seemed to enjoy, thrive, and feed on her ability to manipulate and control the people around her. The fact that she felt no guilt or remorse over her actions is worrisome. The list of potential suspects could get quite long. I am beginning to see the face and the persona of the victim. Now who is the murderer?

CHAPTER NINE

EMMELINE FORTIER

With a fresh cup of coffee in hand I stood for a moment lost in the beauty of the day. A soft scented breeze swept in through the open window and suddenly I was carried into thoughts of simpler times; when summer vacation meant long lazy days, my 1972 Oldsmobile, and endless possibilities. Why was I here and why did I do this? Why had I, and why did I continue to put myself, and worse, my wife and children in harm's way? Did I have something to prove? A flash of movement caught my eye, and when I turned from the window I remembered exactly why I was here. A young girl was murdered and the killer had yet to be caught. It was time for my interview with Emmeline Fortier.

As our eyes met she spoke. Her voice was flat and monotone. "I was given a note and told I needed to see you at ten o'clock." She stood ghostlike in the doorway. Her shoulder length hair was black, framing a pale face with very little makeup. Her thin lips, much like her face carried little color. I thought she appeared sickly and perhaps troubled, yet she looked steadily upon me with the same lifeless grey eyes that I remembered from our first encounter.

"I'm afraid you've caught me dreaming about summer

vacation," I said and then looked toward the clock, "is it ten o'clock already?" I smiled trying to lighten the cool tension that had swept over the room like a small tsunami. It had no effect.

"Five minutes to," she said.

"Please come in Emmeline," I gestured toward the small round table that I used for interviewing, "you didn't attend Muir Middle School did you?"

Emmeline came in and sat down. She folded her hands on the table and met my eye. "No, I went to Highland Middle School, and if it's alright I prefer Emma."

"Alright Emma, first I would like to thank you for finding time to meet with me today. My name is Gilbert Clancy and I work at Muir Middle School as a Student Counselor. I've been asked by my boss Principal James White to conduct a private investigation into the death of Caitlin O'Brien." When I finished she gave me a confused look.

"So you're not with the Police?" She asked in a well-practiced, condescending tone meant to belittle her opponent, and allow her to take charge of the exchange. It implied that for now she would turn off her superior intellect, and lower herself to the level of a silly man who must have thought of himself as Colombo or perhaps Hercule Poirot. I would of course have none of it.

"No, I am not a police officer. As I mentioned earlier, I've been asked to investigate the death of Caitlin O'Brien. I am committed to uncovering the truth, and if I find out that a homicide has occurred, I will make sure that the perpetrator is brought to justice." Tough talk, but she needed to understand I was very serious about my task and not wasting her valuable time.

"What about the police? Rumor has it that Caitlin's death was a murder?" She asked, looking through me with those cold, grey eyes.

"The police are conducting their own investigation. Mine will remain a little more confidential. May we get started with our interview?" I asked.

A sudden chill came over me, and when I looked up, I met the cold and watchful eyes of Monique Fortier. She held my stare for a long moment, almost defying me to turn away. Her expression surprised me; it was one of concern, anger, and maybe even a bit of fear. As I turned back to Emma, I wondered once again what it was that I'd gotten myself into.

"Emma, I know that you are a member of the school's National Honor Society. Caitlin had recently become a member, what did you think about that?"

Emma sat quietly looking at me. I could tell she was nervous and formulating her answer.

"She didn't belong. She never cared about the NHS, and she never showed any interest in our group activities. The National Honor Society is a lot more than a bunch of brainy geeks talking about academics. We do community service, we raise funds for charity, and we work at the school events. Within our membership are the real student leaders of the school. Caitlin became a member for her student resume; another punch on the card." Emma's tone of disdain was strong, and I noted her dislike for Caitlin immediately.

"Emma you are absolutely right. The National Honor Society Chapter of this high school is a model for the rest of the district, and you should be very proud of your membership and service. I was a member of the same chapter many years ago." I paused for a moment, hoping our mutual membership in the same great organization would begin to melt the ice. It didn't, so I went on. "I would like to go back to your earlier comment. You said Caitlin didn't belong. Would you elaborate on that a bit more please?" I glanced at the clock. I needed to keep our interview on track. I knew we didn't have much time before her next class started.

"As I mentioned, we are very proud of the group and our achievements. Most of us have been involved with the NHS since middle school. The fact that Caitlin O'Brien wanted to join, and then became a finalist for the School's Scholarship was a farce. Someone was helping her."

"What kind of service does the National Honor Society do these days?" I asked.

"We manage the school store, run the can drive, deliver meals to the elderly, raise money and purchase gifts for the needy families in the area. We also run the concessions at school events, the profits going to local charities."

As I had hoped, Emma's mood lightened and I caught the slightest hint of a smile as she spoke proudly of the group.

"The work you do is noble and should be celebrated. I need to ask you some more questions about Ms. O'Brien. What I thought I heard you say is that she didn't belong in the NHS. Did she not have the grades?" I asked.

"She had the grades," Emma said. "I sit on the membership committee. We saw her transcripts and then immediately questioned them. We were redirected by Mrs. Vincent, who reminded us that the transcripts are the official record, and that the grades were given by professional teachers, and approved by the school's administrators. She was smart, but she was lazy. She was also very good at cheating. She didn't even hide it. It was as if she was defying anyone to call her out on it. I mentioned it to the teachers so many times that she should have been suspended. My complaints seemed to fall on deaf ears. I believe that someone was watching out for her, someone in the upper echelon of this school or the district."

I leaned back in my chair and thought about how many times I'd heard this same thing, in different forms, from different people. Things were amiss at this school, and I began to believe that those things clearly had something to do with Caitlin's murder. I refocused on Emma and continued the interview. "I know that you are a finalist for the School's Scholarship. It's a well deserved honor and validation for your many years of hard work. As you know there are, or should I say, there were two other finalists."

"One very deserving of the honor, and the other a joke," Emma replied sarcastically, her hatred for the Caitlin and those who had put her in line for the top honor was unmistakable in her tone.

A moment of silence hung between us. I was suddenly taken aback when Emma asked. "Do you know how she died?"

I looked at her for a moment trying to hide my surprise. I

hadn't expected such a direct question from one of the students. We were now trading blows, waiting to see who would be the first to give away their hand. I'd done this too many times in the past, but never with an opponent as cool and calculating as this teenage girl. Now it was my turn. "Yes I do, but that remains confidential. Did your group handle the concessions at the school dance on Saturday night?"

"Yes."

She blinked. I could see her defensive shields beginning to rise.

"I know that Caitlin was there, did you see her?"

"Yes, she was there with Brooke Kincaid and their usual entourage of weak minded boys," Emma replied.

"Did anything strange or unusual happen at the dance?" I asked, hoping that she or a member of the team saw something that might help; an argument, a fight, or someone who didn't belong at the dance.

"No, it was the usual dance. We don't normally have any trouble; we have lots of parent chaperones walking around. My mom was there, you might want to ask her."

"I will thanks." I looked up to find that Monique Fortier and her cart of books to be shelved, hovering within earshot of the conference room.

"What is your job? What concessions do you normally work at the dance and other events?" I asked Emma.

"It depends," she said, "on Saturday night I worked the drink concessions; pop, lemonade, and water."

"Caitlin didn't work the dance?" I asked.

"No, she absolutely refused to work the events. Like I said before, membership in the group was just another check on her resume," Emma replied.

"You mentioned earlier that you thought Caitlin was getting help from someone higher up in the school. Who do you think it was?" Based on my own observations and those of Linda White, I was sure I already knew, but I wanted to hear it from Emma. From what I had learned about Ms. O'Brien's personality, she'd most likely turned on her mentor.

"How confidential is our discussion?" She asked looking around the conference room and library.

I got up from the interview table and closed the office door. "What is said here will not leave this room. If the information you have provided becomes pivotal in the capture of the perpetrator, you can trust I will handle it. Your name will not be revealed."

"I think Principal Baker is behind it," Emma said, her words little more than a whisper. "Caitlin was just another pretty face before he got to the school. He must have been helping her along. The teachers in this school are excellent and very strict. They don't put up with cheating or the other crap she was doing unless they were told to do so. I've also been told that Principal Baker and Caitlin's mom are very close." Emma's face was now flushed, embarrassed to be gossiping. She looked at the clock and then nervously around the library.

"I didn't know that," I said, hoping that my sincerity would cover up my lie.

"Mr. Clancy, I need to get to my next class. Do you have any more questions for me?" Emma asked picking up her backpack.

I stood as she prepared to leave. "No, and thanks again for your time." I extended my hand to her.

Emma took my hand. Her grip was firm and to my surprise her hand was dry. I expected that my line of questioning would have made her nervous. She acted nervous and I thought her hands would confirm it. She was now calm and once again without emotion, just as she had been on our first meeting.

She turned back to me at the conference room door. "Mr. Clancy, I may not have liked Caitlin O'Brien, but the death of any classmate is a terrible thing. It could have been a friend of mine who was killed. Please let me know if I can help." I was surprised at the momentary change and the sincerity in her voice.

"Thanks, you already have. If I have any further questions I'll contact you." I watched her leave. I've spoken face to face with killers before. I had just spent an hour with one of the best I'd ever encountered. I also knew that confident killers stay close to the investigation of their crimes. Suddenly I needed to get out, take a walk, and have a coffee with Sylvia. I also needed to be near my family. My interview with Emmeline Fortier had restored my belief that evil moves about us every day.

CHAPTER TEN

SALVATORE BERTINI

To my great disappointment Brooke Kincaid's mention of a "mobster" reflected on the narrow mindedness of those living in my village. Very soon, if Caitlin's killer was not found, and if I did nothing to avert it, our paranoid community would eventually point its accusatory finger toward my old and dear friend Salvatore Bertini.

Sal is the Owner and Operating Director of The Guild, one of the finest original art studios in the country. The Guild was created by Sal's father Antonio Bertini, who in 1940 left his beloved Sicily seeking refuge in the United States after Mussolini became an ally of Hitler's war machine. With its local manufacturing capacity and talented workforce, Milford made a major contribution to the war effort. Through his dedication and hard work Antonio helped in his own way to defeat the enemy.

In the closing years of the war Milford's prosperity made it attractive to those looking for a better life. The village's economy was better than average with jobs in many of the small mills and manufacturing plants in area. Employees at the time, fresh from the horrors of the Great Depression were desperate for work.

Greedy and immoral businessmen took advantage of the workers with low pay and substandard working conditions. Antonio, a wise and prudent man recognized that employers were growing rich at the expense of their workers. He organized the workers and through his efforts everyone prospered. The workers gained fair and equitable pay, and the plant owners were rewarded with high quality products and loyal employees.

Antonio's unique leadership skills made him the go-to guy when issues could not be resolved. If you had a problem, he would help you solve it. Some were being cheated, others were losing their homes, and others needed advice and assistance starting a business. Antonio always made things right, and in the end, everyone was happy.

Eventually this simple, hard working man became very successful and extremely wealthy. Antonio was a charitable man, a member of the church, and a pillar of the community. It was on a trip back to his beloved Sicily that he rediscovered his love of the arts, and upon his return, The Guild was born.

The Guild occupies a three story building on the village's Main Street. The first floor is an elegant gallery, where an exclusive list of clients purchase original works of art. The building's second floor houses the studio, where the building's original brick walls were reconfigured with floor to ceiling windows, illuminating the artisan's workspace with natural light. Antonio brought Italian masters to Michigan to create sculptures in bronze and marble, many of which adorn important buildings in the Detroit Metropolitan area. Young Salvatore idolized his father, then after graduating from Notre Dame with a degree in Economics he returned home, took over the family business, and started making some real money.

As I reached the building's ornate front facade, a young man in a finely tailored pin stripe suit opened the door and welcomed me inside.

"Good morning Mr. Clancy, it's always a pleasure to see you."

Sergio, at six foot five inches tall and a very solid 275 pounds presented a formidable barrier to anyone threatening the sanctity of the gallery.

"Good Morning Sergio," I extended my hand which he accepted firmly, yet never overpowered despite his obvious size and strength. As always, he was impeccably dressed; the white shirt cuffs that extended just beyond the sleeve of his blue suit jacket were adorned with gold cuff links. His shirt was crisply starched, and he wore a matching paisley tie. His hair was freshly cut and he was clean shaven.

"Mr. Bertini is expecting you. I'll let him know you've arrived."

Sergio stepped away, opened his phone and spoke quietly, nodding his head as Salvatore gave him instructions. A moment later he closed the phone and returned.

"Mr. Bertini will see you now. Do you know the way to his office? I can provide you an escort," Sergio said.

"No need my friend, I know the way."

"Very well Mr. Clancy."

With that I turned to the stairs that would carry me to the building's second floor, and Sergio returned to his duties in the gallery. I smiled and waved to another very large, very well dressed young man named Armand who greeted guests at the gallery's rear entrance. I'd come to learn that these two young men are not only physically impressive, both are academic scholars in the Fine Arts, handpicked by Sal to work in The Guild. Sergio was educated in Venice and Armand was a Loyola graduate. There is no doubt that both were armed with the very best weapons money could buy, and they were amply prepared to dispose of any threat. Together, they represented Sal Bertini's first line of defense.

I ascended the ornamental staircase and found myself standing in a fine studio with ten of the world's best artists. A long wide aisle ran down the center of the work space, at its end a glass door, and beyond that, stairs leading to Sal's office.

"Gilbert, my good friend," I recognized the voice and turned to the smiling face of an olive skinned, heavily mustached Italian sculptor in his work apron. Giorgio was a master in bronze, his talents matched only by a few in the world. His dark hair with streaks of silver, his bright blue eyes, and wide smile were a welcome sight. We'd become close after I helped find his daughter when she ran away from home. I convinced her to come home and stay. I arranged counseling for her, and the family has been happy ever since.

"Good morning Giorgio," I said and offered my hand. He wiped the clay from his own and took it.

"Going to see the boss?" he asked.

"Yes, I need to talk to him," I said.

"You stop by and see me on the way out. Why haven't you come by sooner? Is everything alright, and what about that beautiful wife of yours? I see her walk past everyday on her way to the bookstore," Giorgio said.

I could see that he was hurt that I hadn't kept in touch. "I'll stop back by and we can have a coffee. I would like to see what you are working on."

"Alright," Giorgio smiled and patted me on my shoulder.

I turned toward the far end of the studio and my friend returned to his work. I could hear Sarah Brightman singing low in the background as the mid day sun flooded the studio with light. The smell of clay, the scratching of pencils on paper, and the laughter of the men was energizing. This was much more than just a place to work. These men were friends and a close knit family. As I passed several artists looked up from their work and smiled in greeting. At the end of the studio was the locked glass door which led to Sal's office. Working next to it was an artist whom I was sure represented Sal's second line of defense. To get to the boss you needed his approval.

"Good morning Mr. Clancy," he said wiping the clay from his hands and programmed a code into the electronic keypad. I heard the magnetic lock release and he opened the door for me. I could see the bulge of an automatic weapon under his artist's smock.

"Thank you," I said, looking into dark eyes that watched my every move. This man was responsible for guarding Salvatore's life, and from his expression, he took that responsibility very seriously. I heard the magnetic locks close as I ascended the final steps to Salvatore's office suite which took up the entire third floor of the building.

To my right a door opened into the office of Olympia Tettralini; she'd been Antonio's secretary and now worked for Sal. She smiled as I passed and then returned to her work. The suite that served as Sal's office was paneled in dark cherry wood, with fine leather furniture neatly arranged around a large fireplace. In the open corners of the office stood two exquisite sculptures, from one corner a beautiful life-size winged fairy smiled gracefully upon the visitors, while in the other a bronze bust of Leonardo da Vinci watched the office with an intense stare.

To my right sat a large high tech desk, and behind that stood book shelves overflowing with art and art history books, many of which I had no doubt were original works. On a wall opposite the desk, a large bank of monitors provided Sal with a minute-by-minute view of the gallery, studio, parking garage, rear parking lot, and the gallery's main entrance. A large Sony HD television was tuned to MSNBC. As I watched, the television powered down and paneled wood doors closed off the monitors, I turned to find my good friend entering the room behind me.

"Gilbert," Sal said his arms open in greeting.

Sal Bertini is a man in excellent physical condition and warm and loving to those he considers a friend. At five feet nine inches tall, his imposing form was blessed with broad shoulders, powerful arms, a thick waist, and powerful legs. While in his late forties, I'm sure he would still make an impressive outside linebacker. Sal is also one of those people whose mere presence will instill that sense of calm and control that comes with great leadership. He pulled me into a powerful hug and then stepped back to look at me, a broad smile on his face. I noted that his tailored blue suit fit him perfectly.

"Gilbert, where you been? Too busy to come and see and old friend?"

Somewhat embarrassed I said, "Well, you know how things are with the job and a family?"

"Don't I know it," Sal sighed as he motioned me to sit down in a high backed leather chair. "Can I get you coffee? Have you eaten or would you like a drink?"

"Coffee would be great, thank you," I said.

Sal hit a button on his desk. "Olympia, would you please bring us some coffee."

"Yes, Mr. Bertini."

Sal took his seat on a fine leather couch, crossed his legs, and put one of his muscular arms across the back.

"So my friend, how may I be of service to you?" he asked, his expression serious and back to business.

"I'm investigating the death of Caitlin O'Brien."

Sal shook his head and his eyes dropped for a moment. "Yes, I thought you might be asked to look into it. As you know Giovanni and Caitlin dated last summer. We all fell in love with her and hoped they would someday marry. Alas, you know how children are. My son was hurt when they split, but he has rebounded and is now in love with a nice Sicilian girl."

"Sal, has there been any talk of the O'Brien family within your circle of associates?" My question was direct and to the point. After many years of friendship with Sal Bertini, I've learned that he prefers to deal with everything upfront and head on.

Sal smiled and shook his head, "Gilbert, once again you've demonstrated just how good you really are at this. Yes, there has been a great deal of discussion about the family. You've seen the beautiful home they live in?"

I shook my head. "Oh yes, its size and the location has certainly raised my suspicions."

"Both Mr. and Mrs. O'Brien are well educated and highly successful in their chosen fields, yet they are very foolish people." Sal rose from his seat and moved toward a glass shelved bar which sat to the right of his desk. Without asking he poured two glasses of fine amber Scotch and handed one to me. Then he sat down on the front edge of the couch cushion, his elbows on his knees, and the crystal tumbler cradled in his powerful hands.

"I know that Mr. O'Brien is currently involved in a lucrative business arrangement with a very dangerous associate of mine. I believe that relationship remains sound and extremely profitable for both," Sal commented as Olympia came in and set down a serving tray with the coffee.

"Well that certainly explains the house and the obvious signs of wealth," I said sipping the best Single Malt Scotch Whiskey I'd ever had.

"Gilbert the problem is this. Once you are in with a man like that you are expected to deliver," Sal said taking a generous drink of his Scotch.

"If there was a falling out in the business relationship, do you think that person would kill the daughter to avenge the faults of her father?" I asked. The thought was almost too absurd to consider.

"Gilbert I don't think so," Sal replied in a calm tone that contrasted greatly with the concerned look on his face, "families and most certainly children are off limits. However, depending upon the amount of damage the father's indiscretion has done, my associate may have broken that most sacred of rules. Heaven help him should I discover that he has committed such a heinous act. This type of thing simply cannot happen in my village."

As I watched Sal's darker side reveal itself for the briefest of moments, I realized just how fortunate I was to have him on my side.

CHAPTER ELEVEN

COMPARING NOTES

My investigation into the death of Caitlin O'Brien was now into its fourth day, and I was no closer to a solution than I was on day one. After leaving Sal Bertini's office I stopped at the village Starbucks, sat at an outside table, and watched people walk by as I contemplated my next move. I pulled my laptop from its bag and reviewed the balance of the download from Caitlin's table. As I expected there were no smoking guns and no red flags.

In keeping with the tradition of all great detectives, I tapped out the basic question on my keyboard. *What do I know so far?*

Caitlin and Brooke were at the school dance on Saturday night. Afterward, they went out and got home very late. Brooke hadn't noticed that Caitlin was tired or not feeling well.

Then I recalled what Sylvia said about poison. "The perfect poison is tasteless in its delivery. It must be carefully selected and then configured to delay its effect, allowing considerable time and distance to separate the killer from their victim." It was quite obvious that this killer knew exactly what he or she was doing.

I returned to my case notes.

Based on my interviews and observations at the funeral home, Caitlin O'Brien made more than her fair share of enemies along the way, but not the kind of enemies capable of committing murder. So far the investigation has uncovered lots of motive, some deep insight into the persona of Caitlin O'Brien, and some really nasty skeletons in a number of closets, but nothing concrete. Was Caitlin just another troublemaking teenager or perhaps the victim of a professional hit, because her father was drawn into the alluring game of illicit wealth?

And why would Richard Baker risk it all to fast track Caitlin into the School's Scholarship? The days of timid, easily silenced employees are over, especially in professional educators whose lives revolve around honesty and academic integrity. There was far too much risk from a whistleblower. Furthermore, did an affair with Pam O'Brien mean so much that he was willing to throw away his reputation, position at the school, and standing in the community? That seemed highly unlikely; Baker is undoubtedly a man who likes to be in charge. If he did violate the community's trust, I will make sure he is called upon to answer for it.

Both Sylvia and Bobby have suggested that Caitlin's mother should be considered a suspect. If Pam O'Brien was involved, it will eventually come out. Having children of my own, I've respected the family's need to mourn and will see them later today. What of the father's dealings with, as Sal had put it, a very dangerous associate? Had he simply discounted this man as just another supplier to the company, another small business hungry for work, and easily manipulated? Was it a mistake that cost Caitlin her life?

Emma Fortier continues to concern me. She seems too cold to be affected by the guilt that eventually uncovers the amateur murderer. I have the impression that she thinks she is too smart to get caught. To this point she is grossly in error. Even the very best make one small mistake, and that's all I need.

I stopped typing and looked up as Bobby Thomas's car pulled up to the curb. He drove a very plain black Chevy Impala that said police car all over it. He walked up and took a seat at the table. The sun was bright and he was wearing wraparound Oakley Sunglasses.

"Gil, how you doing?" he asked and then motioned to someone in the shop to bring him some coffee.

"They already know what you want?" I asked smiling sarcastically as my friend appeared to be taking full advantage of his position with the police force.

"My friend this is the modern day donut shop. I do some of my best thinking here," Bobby explained as an attractive young lady brought him a Tall Vanilla Latte.

"Thanks dear," Bobby said and smiled as she set the coffee down in front of him. He tipped the barista named Kimberly very well, and I watched her look back over her shoulder at him before going inside the building.

"Lovely girl isn't she," Bobby commented as the glass doors closed and Kimberly disappeared.

"A Vanilla Latte," I asked in feigned confusion, "what happened to that black gut rot coffee that all you great detectives are supposed to drink?"

"Starbucks, baby," Bobby raised his cup in praise.

I joined him. I had to admit that Starbucks had become quite a cultural phenomenon.

"What do you know so far?" Bobby asked and then relaxed in his chair, sunglasses pushed up on his forehead, and sipping happily on his coffee.

I told him about my interviews and my discussion with Salvatore Bertini, which I reminded him, was completely off the record. As promised, I held back specific details from my interviews with Brooke and Emma. Bobby appreciated and benefitted from the information that I brought to the investigation. Since most, if not all of it would never be admissible in a court; he treated it as an anonymous tip. With our usual understanding in place, I proceeded with my report while he sat quietly and drank his coffee, listening closely to everything I said.

When I finished he spoke. "Based on your discussion with Sal, do you think O'Brien is taking kickbacks? Some of those contracts can be worth millions. People have certainly been killed for a lot less."

"Look at the house they live in. I don't make enough in one year to pay the property taxes on it for god sakes!" I said, suddenly embarrassed at what surely sounded like whining.

Bobby glanced back at me with a look of insincere skepticism and a sarcastic smile.

"You know what I mean."

"I do, and I think we need to review their financial records and chase down all that money. Find the source of the money and we might just find our killer. I can take care of that," Bobby said and smiled as Kimberly came out with a fresh coffee for both of us. Hanging out with a cop does have its advantages.

"There is one more thing." Bobby set down his coffee and walked to his illegally parked police car. He returned with a manila envelope and laid it on the table. "Toxicologist report is back. Caitlin O'Brien died after ingesting a poison cocktail made from a high concentration of Rhubarb extract and Isopropanol. She must have been very sick and suffered excruciating pain before she died. It is amazing that she was able to drive her car at all."

"Rhubarb and Isopropanol definitely complicates things. There is certainly an abundance of rhubarb around and Isopropanol; rubbing alcohol, window cleaner, eye glass lens cleaner..." I ticked off the possible sources until I ran out of fingers.

"That covers the means. Now we need to find the motive, and most important the opportunity," Bobby said as he slipped into thought about the case.

"Sylvia is convinced that the presence of poison suggests that our killer is a woman," I said.

Bobby returned from where ever he was and looked at me, "How so?"

Trying not to steal my brilliant wife's thunder I launched into my explanation. "Poison is the perfect weapon for a woman. First, there is no physical contact. Second, if she chooses and then formulates the poison correctly, its effects are mistaken for a simple illness; a migraine headache or perhaps the flu. Third, she is smart enough to choose a poison or poisons that can be extracted from common everyday products. This is not the crime of an amateur, and most certainly not a crime of passion. The question that remains to be answered is this. When, where, and how did our killer actually poison Caitlin?" Even as I asked the question, I was quite sure I already knew the answer.

Bobby turned back to his folder. "The Coroner has determined by the amount of organ damage, the concentration of acetone; which is the metabolized isopropyl alcohol in the body, and the metabolic rate of a healthy seventeen year old girl, she was given the poison sometime Saturday night."

If I accepted the fact that Caitlin was poisoned at the dance, there could be hundreds of potential suspects. Of the many who hated her, who could actually pull it off? Suddenly the image of Emmeline Fortier flashed before my mind's eye. Could it be that easy? The simple answer is no, because I would have to prove beyond doubt that she acquired the rhubarb plants, understood the process and then intentionally extracted the poison from the leaves, then delivered that poison to Caitlin at the dance.

"Gil, you still with me," Bobby asked.

His voice brought me back from troubled thoughts and I turned to meet his eye. "We now understand how she was killed, when she was poisoned, and where she was poisoned, what still bothers me is why was she poisoned? Why did she have to die?"

CHAPTER TWELVE

THE MANOR

I left the asphalt and pulled onto a manicured gravel drive. The gentle sound of stones under my tires brought back memories of simpler times, when most of the roads around the village were still gravel. Overhead, the canopies of trees created a tunnel of green and shadow and light. Beyond, the grounds of the estate treated its visitors to a tapestry of color. Gardens of every shape and size formed a colorful patchwork on the rolling green lawn. Some, I noted, formed the border of a fish pond, and in others, figures of bronze and stone stood like sentinels over their domain. The one common feature of all the gardens was the lavender colored blooms. The trees gave way to a wide flat expanse of lawn, and the Manor House came into view.

The beauty and distinctive feature of the French Provincial style is its adherence to symmetry. The home that stood before me was an exquisite example of that design. The long Limestone and Blue Slate walk leading to the house, afforded those interested with an opportunity to study and appreciate a style of architecture that originated in Sixteenth Century southern France.

The steep gabled roof was covered with blue slate tiles very

similar in color and texture to those under foot. Contrasting the blue of the tiles, copper roof valleys gave your eye a logical path to follow in the sea of slate. The valleys led to bright, gracefully executed copper gutters that divided the roof from the front façade of the home. The gutters eventually emptied into symmetrically placed downspouts that naturally directed your eye back to the center of the limestone home.

The arched front doors sat in a covered alcove. On each side of the recess were tall arched windows. On the left one could see a formal sitting room, and on the right, the home's library. One step up placed the visitor on a small but elegant courtyard. Sculpted balustrades supported a limestone railing that separated the boundaries of the home from the grounds. A few more steps brought me to the arched front doors. Just as I reached for a brass knocker that closely resembled a flying pig, the door opened and I stood face to face with Pamela O'Brien.

I don't know why, but I expected her to greet me with a heavily accented "Bonjour." My mind is funny that way, and I tried to hide my disappointment when she said in English, "Mr. Clancy, it is very nice to see you again, please come in."

In shades of yellow, lavender, and blue, the house that Caitlin had called home was grand indeed. My South of France fantasy was shattered when I remembered that some, if not all of this had come from illegal activities.

"Mr. Clancy if you'll follow me to the kitchen, I've made coffee and we can talk."

We sat in a breakfast nook that overlooked a terrace that was identical to the front, only flipped about the home's center line. Where would we be without symmetry?

"Mr. Clancy, I owe you an apology," Mrs. O'Brien said while pouring coffee from a porcelain carafe. "I was not very nice to you on the night of Caitlin's visitation. We were so blessed and overjoyed by the number of guests and outpouring of love. Unfortunately when you and a number of other guests arrived to extend your much appreciated condolences, I was distracted, watching for my brother. He was scheduled to arrive with our

75

mother. She and Caitlin were very close and I was very worried about her condition."

I looked at the sincerity in her eyes, and suddenly I wanted to forget that this woman might have committed the act that brought us together today.

"Now Mr. Clancy, how can I help you?"

I looked at Pamela O'Brien wondering how she could be so pleasant just days after what should have been the very worst day of her life. Was it an act, or was it because a great burden was lifted from her shoulders? Had Caitlin's death spared her from another type of pain?

"First, I must again extend to you my deepest condolences for your loss. Caitlin's death was a loss to all that knew her. I knew her well when she was a student in my school. Other members of the staff and I celebrated her success, and truly looked forward to the incredible young woman she would someday become."

"Thank you," she said and reached for a tissue to dry the tears welling in her eyes.

"May I ask, what were Caitlin's plans for college?"

"Caitlin was accepted to Stanford, Yale, and Notre Dame. We expected her final decision right after graduation," Mrs. O'Brien said dabbing at her tears.

"I know she was a finalist for the School's Scholarship. Did that have any influence on where she would attend college?"

"No, we'd already decided that if she won, it would be donated to a more deserving student. My husband and I had already made all the preparations for Caitlin's college."

"That is a very kind and generous gesture," I said as an awkward moment of quiet hung between us.

"Mrs. O'Brien, the better I understand your daughter, the better chance I have to catch the person responsible for this. With your permission I would like to examine her room."

"Of course you have my permission. I'll do anything to catch the person who took her from me."

"Thank you, and finally I'll need to interview you and then Mr. O'Brien. I prefer to interview you separately, because some of my questions might be embarrassing for one or both of you." My final statement seemed to be the tipping point. For the slightest moment her expression changed to one of surprise and panic. As I suspected, she had something to hide.

Then just as quickly she was back. "If you have no more questions, I can take you to Caitlin's room now." She rose from her seat at the table and I followed.

"Please take all the time you need," Mrs. O'Brien said leaving me to my work.

The room was lilac in color and the furniture contemporary. A queen size bed, dresser, chest of drawers, and amore were white. On a stand in the corner was a large flat screen television, and on the nightstand an Ipod speaker. The suite reflected the style and grandeur of the home with a walk-in closet and private bath. It felt strange to stand in the room, seeing it the same way Caitlin had in the final moments of her life, very ill and in dire need of life saving medical treatment.

Bobby's team had already been to the house, examined the suite, taken pictures, and collected forensic samples. The O'Brien's had not cleaned the room since their daughter's death, entering only to gather the funeral clothing and jewelry. I stepped into the bathroom with its long cluttered vanity, toilet, shower, and whirlpool tub. It smelled of perfume and scented body wash. Dried vomit and blood remained untouched on the floor, toilet and wall; a reminder of Caitlin's last minutes.

I stood for some time in the quiet of the room, retracing the girl's final hours in my mind. She woke in the early hours of Sunday morning with flu like symptoms. She was sore and her stomach was upset, she had a pounding headache and so dizzy she could barely stand. Her mouth and throat burned, which she would have blamed on earlier bouts of throwing up.

As the hours passed she felt worse. She drifted in and out of a troubled sleep, finally waking when the need to vomit overcame all else. I looked from the bed to the bathroom. I could see items that were once on the dresser scattered about the floor. Most likely she'd stumbled or fallen against it in her attempts to get to the bathroom. Caitlin barely reached the toilet before being sick, which explained the bloody splatter on the wall. She called to her parents from the floor of the bathroom and no one came to her aid. Perhaps they didn't hear her over the expanse of space, most likely they weren't home.

Somehow she pulled on clothes, staggered down the stairs, through the house, and got into her car. She was confused as the poison's effects ravaged her body, so instead of calling for help, she decided to go to Brooke's. I stepped to a window that overlooked the front yard. I could see where her car left the gravel drive and entered the yard. She narrowly missed a large pond, and then ran into a stone bench which lay toppled and broken from the encounter. Somehow she managed to thread her car between two very large oak trees and reenter the drive. I can only imagine how the final minutes played out before her life ended, almost three miles away and directly in front of Sylvia's bookstore.

From the bathroom window I could see the balance of the O'Briens' property as it faded into the forests of Kensington Metro Park. From the limestone terrace, the yard stepped down in colorful tiers to the swimming pool. There was no indication that any of the flower gardens had been altered, or evidence of plants having been recently dug up. I was certain that if Bobby's team had found anything this case would be closed.

In the corner of Caitlin's room, opposite the tall armoire was a desk. On its work space sat a Dell flat screen monitor, keyboard, and wireless mouse. Schoolbooks sat on one corner. The thick layer of dust confirmed that they hadn't been opened for some time. I sat down, moved the mouse, and the sleeping monitor came to life. Like her tablet, computer security was not a concern to Caitlin and the desktop appeared. I began my investigation with a search of her documents.

I found a few English assignments, notes from the National Honor Society and letters to a much admired boyfriend. Where were all the research papers and homework assignments? A National Honor Society member and candidate for the School's Scholarship should have been swimming in work and research material. I opened and closed desk drawers, there were no hard paper copies, compact disks, or flash drives. This was all wrong. Morgan was buried in schoolwork, and our family's home computer in constant use.

A search of the spreadsheet program revealed some math, accounting, and science homework, but not nearly enough to suggest that this girl was an academic scholar. The fast tracking story began to make more sense, but why? The door swung quietly open and Pam O'Brien entered the room. Her expression said that she was concerned and very uncomfortable with my investigation.

"Mr. Clancy, is everything alright? Can I help you with anything?" she asked in the welcoming tone I'd heard earlier.

"Yes, I'm hoping you can help with a few things. Mrs. O'Brien, your daughter was a member of the school's National Honor Society and a finalist for the School's Scholarship, yet I cannot find evidence of a normal level of schoolwork, let alone that of a scholar. Did Caitlin have another computer? Or has someone deleted files from this computer? I'm troubled because I guess I would have expected to find more." By now, I felt a great dislike for Mrs. O'Brien and left out the niceties in my tone and words.

She looked surprised and then appalled at my line of questioning. "No, Caitlin had her computer and tablet, if she completed homework on the computer, it would be there. Perhaps the police took the compact disks or the flash drives for further investigation. Otherwise, I really don't know where else it would be." Then she quickly changed the subject. "I spoke to my husband. He'll be home in about forty five minutes if you would still like to talk with him." Then without another word, she turned and left me alone again.

Sylvia had always considered my methods cruel. On the other hand, I felt that I gained a psychological advantage when a potential suspect was left to stew over their emotions, worrying about some small detail they may have missed, and one that I would most certainly find. I pulled my own flash drive from my pocket and made copies of all of Caitlin's documents, and then a copy of all email messages. I was certain that Bobby's forensic team had done the same. I was surprised that the computer was still here.

I completed my look into the private life of Caitlin O'Brien with a general walk through her room. The family certainly knew how to spend the extra money Mr. O'Brien received from the alleged kickbacks. Pictures on the dresser showed Caitlin skiing in Colorado and Banff, Canada. Another showed the golden hues of fall in Vermont as a backdrop for Caitlin and her mother, both smiling in front of a bright red covered bridge. There were at least half a dozen pictures of her in formal dresses, standing with a smiling date. Another showed a younger Caitlin next to her first car. In another, she stood next to the silver Cobalt SS, her last car. In the final picture of the collection I saw Caitlin and her friends standing in front of a Provence Chateau with rolling hills of lavender in the background.

Then I turned, worked up my courage, and entered the walk-in closet. Most men cower away from this challenge, but I stood tall and took one for the team. Flipping on the light switch I wasn't disappointed, Caitlin had a vast collection of clothes. What I was looking for was tucked away in the back of the cavernous closet, hidden behind a tall stack of shoeboxes. It was a manila envelope full of newspaper clippings. It contained every newspaper article and picture that Caitlin had ever appeared in. The October 23, 2008 Milford Gazette carried a story titled:

Art Teacher goes too far

Jonathon Peters; long time art and jewelry teacher at Milford High School has been suspended indefinitely, pending charges of inappropriate conduct with a student. Caitlin O'Brien and her parents, Pamela and Jacob have called for Mr. Peters' dismissal and will seek criminal charges. The O'Brien's are also seeking an undisclosed

amount for damages from the school district.
"Jonathon Peters is one of the finest, most
professional educators that I've had the
pleasure to work with and has my full
support. I am certain that he will be
exonerated of all charges," said Helen
Bulla, Principal of Milford High School.
Peters has an estranged wife and teenage
daughter Emmeline neither was available for
comment.

I put the manila folder away and wandered back through the O'Brien house in a daze. Emmeline was not a common name; I wondered if it could be Emmeline Fortier that the article made reference too? Had Monique Fortier once been married to Jonathon Peters? Only in a small town I thought, finding Pamela O'Brien completing some paperwork in her office.

She looked up as I reached the office door.

"Mr. Clancy, please sit down. Did you learn anything new?" Pamela O'Brien asked.

"Yes I did, and I would like to thank you for the opportunity to do so during these most difficult of times. Mrs. O'Brien, do you have time for our interview?"

"Yes, of course." Her look was one of confidence, she was certain I hadn't found anything.

"Mrs. O'Brien, before we begin can you tell me, was there a specific food or drink that was a favorite of your daughter's? Something she ate or drank consistently?"

"Lemonade, Caitlin loved lemonade. We always had it in the house and she always drank it when we went out, why would you ask that Mr. Clancy?"

"I am looking for a pattern. Something the suspect noticed, or paid attention to that presented them with an opportunity to poison to your daughter."

I paused for a moment, looked into Pamela O'Brien's calm and confident eyes, certain that my next line of questioning was about to change that. "Mrs. O'Brien, I believe that your daughter's death has something to do with the school. She was a member of the National Honor Society and a finalist for the School's Scholarship. As I mentioned earlier, I've seen no evidence that demonstrates any level of strenuous academic workload. I would have expected her locker, desk, and room to be covered with schoolwork and research, and yet, I found nothing. I also have my suspicions that Richard Baker orchestrated her ascension. I cannot prove that, but others share in my opinion. He used his influence to fast track Caitlin to her nomination for the school's scholarship, and he did it because he's in love with you." I stopped and waited for Pamela O'Brien's reaction to such a harsh accusation.

She smiled and then looked away, my accusations were true. A long moment of silence hung between us before she spoke in a tone that was all business.

"Mr. Clancy, it is true that Richard and I have had an on-again, off-again relationship. I don't know how you discovered that, but I am sure it's part of the investigation. What do you think that has to do with my daughter's death?"

"Are you on-again or off-again?" I asked

"We are on-again," she said with a shade of color to her face.

"Did Caitlin know about your relationship?"

"She was a bright girl, I'm sure she probably knew. She liked Richard and really appreciated his advice and counsel."

"Mrs. O'Brien, Caitlin never confronted you? Wasn't she concerned about how your affair might be hurting her father? Did she ever confront Baker about the affair?" I decided that she and I had volleyed with small talk long enough. It was time to press her a bit.

"Caitlin and I never spoke about the affair. As I mentioned before, she was a very smart and perceptive girl. She also lived in this house and knew firsthand the type of relationship my husband and I have. She never confronted me or Richard about the affair." As she said this a small chime sounded in the house.

"That must be Jacob. You can wait for him in his study. Double doors, next to the sitting room." Then, without another word Mrs. O'Brien put her glasses back on and returned to her work. I was dismissed from her office. I turned and made my way through the O'Brien house to the study where I waited for Jacob O'Brien.

CHAPTER THIRTEEN

JACOB O'BRIEN

Jacob O'Brien's study was just as I pictured it, with dark paneled walls, bookshelves adorned with leather bound books, Terry Redlin paintings, fine leather furniture, an enormous desk, and a stone fireplace. In the corner of the room stood an executive bar, mirrored and backlit shelves displayed Waterford crystal decanters filled with various colored liquors. My eye was drawn to a decanter of amber colored fluid that could be nothing else but a Single Malt Scotch.

When Jacob O'Brien entered through the study's double doors, I stood and he offered his hand. "Mr. Clancy, my wife tells me that you are assisting with the investigation into Caitlin's death."

O'Brien's handshake was firm and his blue eyes were sincere. Though I clearly understood that he didn't play the game of life fairly, I felt for his loss, and found that I liked him. He stepped over to the bar and filled two crystal tumblers with the fine amber colored Scotch. He handed me one and then sat down in a large leather chair.

"Yes, I've been asked by James White, the Principal of Muir Middle School to look into this. We both knew Caitlin and celebrated her success. Her passing brought great sorrow to the staff of the school, and we wanted to provide whatever assistance we can. My investigation is private in nature, but I am communicating with the detective in charge." As I said this, I watched Mr. O'Brien draw off half of his tumbler, and then return to the bar, and refill his glass.

"Mr. Clancy, what can I do to help?" O'Brien pulled the double doors to the study closed and then returned to his seat.

"Mr. O'Brien, as I explained to your wife, my investigation is being done on the direct order of my boss as a representative of the school district. Everything you say will be held in the greatest of confidence."

"Understood," O'Brien replied as a calm rosy glow settled across his cheeks.

"With the death of a child, an investigator worth their stuff must first look to the parents; their home, their careers, and their lifestyles. Honestly, there are things here that just don't add up." I gestured at the opulence of the richly adorned study. "This does not make sense. I understand that you and Mrs. O'Brien are very successful in your respective careers, but this type of wealth is over the top. I am sure that the police have asked the same questions looking for a possible link." I watched for O'Brien's reaction. He took another full drink from his tumbler and then to my surprise, he met my eye.

"Mr. Clancy, as you already know my wife is very successful in the Real Estate business, and I'm an Executive Director with an automobile company. We have a very good income. We have saved our money, invested well, and profitably bought and sold properties."

"Mr. O'Brien, with all due respect, this fabulous home cost millions of dollars. Your neighbors are very successful business owners, many of them millionaires in their own right, and you are not. However, I believe that you have another source of income." Jacob O'Brien's expression was now one of concern.

I went on. "A reliable source has told me that you are receiving kickbacks from some of the suppliers that provide parts for your company's assembly plants." I thought he would argue in his own defense, or at least throw me out, but that did not come. Instead, his shoulders slumped and his face became ashen. All that I had confronted him with was true.

"Yes, Mr. Clancy. I have received millions of dollars in kickbacks from multiple suppliers. It was tough the first time I accepted it. Then it just got easier, and soon it became a common business practice. Things were going very well, and I had it under control until a certain gentleman, if you can call him that entered the supplier base. First it was dinner invitations to the Detroit Yacht Club, and then the best seats at the Joe. Then he began to reel me in. We'd become friends, which was my first mistake. I felt comfortable with him and his company did great work." He stopped to finish his Scotch.

"It started when one of my engineers screwed up. It would have shut down a major assembly plant on one of our best product lines. It would have cost the company millions a day."

O'Brien's gaze drifted from me and focused on a spot somewhere in the middle of the floor. "I met with him right away, told him what had happened, and he told me not to worry. They changed all the tooling without charging me. They worked around the clock, revalidated the parts, and kept the plant going. I was so grateful that I began pushing more and more work his way.

His company continued to do a great job and everyone prospered. I was truly happy for his success. He bailed me out a number of times after that. Then he invited me to go golfing up north. When I got to my room, I found an envelope on the desk. He had written on it; *A little token of my appreciation*. It was a $10,000.00 deposit to my checking account. I told him that I could not accept it. He insisted that his success was all due to the opportunity I'd provided them.

We began to notice more deposits. We weren't sure how he was able to gain access to our accounts. Then we accepted the big gift, the title to the land that this house sits on. After we moved into our beautiful new home, his friendly business calls became orders. It seemed that I was now working for him. His sales reps would show up with a request for more work, and "no" was not an option. I called him and tried to end it. I told him that I would turn over the house, the land, and all the money over to him. He said we'd come too far for that.

When I told him that I had turned in my resignation to the company, he told me to withdraw it or terrible things would begin happening to my family. So I stayed."

I could see that Jacob O'Brien wanted to tell someone this for a long time. I stood, refilled our glasses, and handed his back to him. "Mr. O'Brien, do you think this man had anything to do with the death of your daughter?" I asked, leaning forward to catch his eye.

"With new leadership in the company, more of the work is being sent off-shore," O'Brien said, his voice now low and exhausted. "Machiavelli told me to keep the work coming. When I told him that it was now out of my hands, he hung up the phone. I figured that within days I'd be dead, and to be honest Mr. Clancy I didn't care."

"Mr. O'Brien when did Machiavelli make that threat?" I asked.

"Two weeks before Caitlin died," O'Brien said and then broke down sobbing into his hands, certain that his greed had led to the death of his only child.

I reached over and laid a hand on his shoulder. "I will find out what happened to Caitlin. If Machiavelli had something to do with it, he will be brought to justice. If he did not kill your daughter, he will still be brought forward to answer for the extortion. What is this man's name and where is his company?"

"Anthony Machiavelli. The name of the company is European Mold and Manufacturing. It's in Troy, on Stephenson Highway," O'Brien said wiping his cheeks with his handkerchief, before emptying the tumbler of Scotch in a shaky swallow.

"Thank you Mr. O'Brien." I said and set my glass down on the desk.

As I left O'Brien's study, I glanced across the vast formal living room into Pamela O'Brien's office and met her eye. She was trying to read my expression, trying to understand what I knew. I didn't like her, and it would take an irrefutable confession from another before I would believe she didn't have something to do with this. As for Anthony Machiavelli, I would need another consultation with Sal Bertini.

CHAPTER FOURTEEN

THE CAMERA NEVER LIES

"This is a messy one," Sylvia said as we sat down to dinner.

"Yes it is. In addition to all the issues surrounding Caitlin, Mrs. O'Brien is having an affair with Richard Baker. Should it be revealed, it would of course ruin them both," I said looking across the table at my beautiful wife who now gave me her full attention. She had prepared what I like to call my "Green Mile Meal," orzo pasta with spinach and salmon. The meal I would ask for if it was my last.

"Jacob O'Brien on the other hand has made a substantial fortune in kickbacks from suppliers to his company. Things were going very well until he met a man named Machiavelli, who has turned the tables on him. A change in company policy is pushing more work off-shore and less is available for local suppliers, which means that Jacob O'Brien isn't holding up his end of the bargain. He is certain that Machiavelli had Caitlin killed in retaliation. With that said, I still don't understand why? What benefit does he gain from that? He could have easily destroyed O'Brien professionally and then move on."

"People have been killed for a lot less," Sylvia added."

"Yes they have, but why have the girl killed when you know that all roads lead to Sal Bertini?"

Sylvia smiled back at me and shook her head. She understands Sal Bertini and the role he plays in our small community.

"Even if Machiavelli had her killed, why would a professional hit man do it with poison? Why not make a clean job of it and simply make her disappear? I don't believe he's the guy. As you have suggested," I added, smiling and bowing my head slightly to acknowledge my wife's deductive brilliance. "This one was personal, between Caitlin and her killer. The poison was given to her at the dance. A complete stranger would have drawn too much attention. The killer was a student, a chaperone, or someone's date." When I finished my assessment I looked at Sylvia. She was smiling at me, I must be on the right track.

"You could find that out easy enough."

"How," I asked.

"Pictures and security video; with the issues of the day, doors are locked and security cameras run twenty four hours a day in the schools. Security upgrades were part of the last millage vote," Sylvia informed me.

I looked at her. How did she remember these things? Come to think of it I guess I did notice a bit more security at the Middle School.

"I am certain that every person coming in and going out of that dance was recorded, and most didn't even know it," she said.

"I thought of that," I said in my own defense.

"No, you didn't," she said.

"You're right, I didn't." I returned to my dinner, and when I looked up she was still smiling at me. I winked and blew her a kiss.

"The murderer could still be one of the students or a member of the staff," I said. "Caitlin was very popular. She did some pretty interesting things; some good, most bad, and she made a lot of enemies. That deal with Jonathon Peters was very bad business and lots of people got hurt." Suddenly I was tired of talking about

Caitlin O'Brien.

Picking up on my change in mood, Sylvia said in passing. "There's a lot to clean up on this one."

Much to my daughter's objections, we found ourselves at the high school on Saturday morning reviewing the security tapes from the dance. Morgan felt that she should be paid for this work since it was well above and beyond the requirements of her normal chores. I assured my daughter that her reward would far exceed the sacrifices she was making.

On the monitor we watched members of staff, the custodial crew, and the disc jockey and her roadies come and go. Soon after the adult chaperones and National Honor Society members showed up early to complete their set up. The camera at the door revealed nothing out of the ordinary, and with Morgan's help I took note of those students whose dates did not attend the school. I paid special attention to those with older dates, men and women.

"Did you get a chance to review the camera in the cafeteria?" Vice Principal Beckett asked.

"No, we didn't," I answered over Morgan's icy stare. Her Saturday was going fast and the reward I'd promised would be costly. "We'll hurry through it," I assured her.

The recording was very clear, given the darkness of the cafeteria, the flashing lights, and the rapidly moving people. The camera, which sat inside a shatterproof bubble was fastened to the ceiling, rotated slowly and captured the entire room. I stopped the recording when I saw Morgan and her date a little closer than I would have liked, then took great pleasure in the color that flushed in her cheeks.

The concessions and a small café were set up for eating, drinking, and talking in an area outside the reach of the loud music. Coolers full of pop, water and other soft drinks were lined up on tables. I saw a few fountain dispensers, one with orange, and the other with lemonade. I also had a clear image of Emmeline Fortier serving drinks and supporting the efforts of the National Honor Society.

To Morgan's relief we finished only thirty minutes later than I had planned. I thanked Mr. Beckett for his time and joined my daughter in the car. We drove quietly southeast on I-96 toward Novi and the Mall. Morgan would now receive her reward. I was caught up in my thoughts and she on her new iPhone. I was certain that I had just identified the killer's opportunity to deliver the poison. My hands were shaking when I reached up and took the key from the ignition.

CHAPTER FIFTEEN

POISONED DRINKS

I've learned from my wife and two daughters that the best place to be during a woman's shopping spree is out of the way. To more easily facilitate that exchange of commerce, the marketing people and the interior designers of the Twelve Oaks Mall had once more demonstrated their brilliance. Knowing that the presence of a bored, uncomfortable man might cause a female customer to rush through the store, resulting in a loss of maximum revenue, they created a diversion. Strategically placed couches, chairs, and flat screened televisions are placed in living room type arrangements outside many of the most popular stores so that the "driver" has some place to comfortably hang out with those of his kind and wait. To my great relief one of those "arrangements" was located just outside Banana Republic. While Morgan searched the store, I sat and thought about what I'd seen on the security tapes of the dance.

While the security camera offered a comprehensive view of the scene, what I really needed were more finite details. I pulled the cell phone from my pocket and began searching for a specific number.

"Hello," Linda White answered not recognizing the number being displayed on the caller ID.

"Linda, this is Gilbert," I said.

"Hi Gilbert, what's up?"

"Did you have a yearbook photographer at the dance on Saturday?"

"Yes I did, does this have anything to do with Caitlin O'Brien?"

"It does. Would it be possible for me to see all the photos taken that night? I'm pretty sure that the school has become our crime scene." The phone went silent for a moment. "Linda, are you still there?"

"Yes Gil, I'm still here. Are you suggesting that someone at the dance may have caused Caitlin's death?"

"Yes, I believe she was poisoned at the dance."

The phone was silent for a long time before Linda spoke. "Kid's name is Austin Bayley. He's a freshman, very good photographer, and he uses the latest equipment. I'll have him drop of the memory card at Sylvia's store. He lives just a couple of blocks from there."

"Thank you," I said knowing that she would call Austin and then pick up the memory card herself to ensure its safe delivery.

"Let me know if there is anything else I can do," Linda said and then the connection broke.

By the time Morgan and I got home dinner was ready. Sylvia was home early, she'd hired a few assistants to keep the store open later on the weekends.

"Linda dropped off a package for you at the store. I put it on your desk," she said as I pulled the door shut and Morgan went in to show Sylvia her new things.

The package was one of those mailing envelopes with bubble wrap to protect the contents. I opened it and found that Austin had burned a CD I could keep. I put the CD in the computer and selected the first image. In slide show mode, I moved quickly through the pictures. I saw many of the people I'd seen at the funeral, including the same three girls who had viciously scorned Caitlin while looking so remorseful.

Dressed in more casual attire, the school's faculty members

were smiling and looked like they were really having a good time. The next photo caused my blood to run cold as Caitlin O'Brien smiled back at the camera. She and Brooke sat close together, their pretty smiling faces illuminating the shot. Had she already been poisoned by the time this picture was taken? I studied the other photos until I found one with the clock in clear view; it showed ten thirty five, the dance would end at eleven o'clock.

I went back to the photo of Caitlin. Now over my immediate shock, I began to notice other details. She and Brooke were seated in the café area. On the table before them were drinks; Caitlin had her usual lemonade and Brooke with an Evian water. There was a third drink, and what caught my eye was the way its owner had carefully wrapped a napkin around the cup. The fingers that held the drink were nicely shaped; the nails were colored a shade of burgundy and professionally done. On her right hand, she wore a Milford class ring.

I could tell by the angle of the hand that she was seated at the table. I scanned the rest of the pictures hoping to get a better look at the mystery girl, who also appeared to be drinking lemonade. In my search for the third girl, I found a smiling picture of Emma Fortier. She'd been caught in the act of filling a cup of ice from the lemonade fountain. I looked at the picture for a long time, wondering how the killer poisoned Caitlin. Would she have been bold enough to try it in clear view of the students? Or was the poison put in the cup by a 'friend' who brought them drinks? Beyond the smiles and the drinks I could see Monique Fortier standing watch over the activities. It suddenly dawned on me that I hadn't seen her come in or leave the building that night. All attendees should have been caught on the security cameras.

I picked up my school directory from the desk, opened it and dialed Brooke Kincaid's number.

"Hello," Mrs. Kincaid answered.

"Mrs. Kincaid, this is Gilbert Clancy from Muir Middle School. I am very sorry to be calling you at dinner time on Saturday night, but this is very important. May I please speak to Brooke?"

"No problem at all Mr. Clancy. You and I spoke often when

Brooke was at Muir. She was…" Mrs. Kincaid paused for a moment, "difficult."

"It's a tough time for all kids," I assured her, "your daughter has become a fine young woman, and we spoke at length the other day. I don't know if she told you but I have been asked to look into the death of Caitlin O'Brien."

"That was tragic," Mrs. Kincaid said, "Brooke's been a mess since it happened. She lost her best friend, and then with the circumstances behind it, just awful. Mr. Clancy, Brooke is not here, but I can give you her cell phone number. If she doesn't answer let me know and I'll call her back. She knows better than to ignore my call."

"Alright, thanks so much Mrs. Kincaid." With the number in hand I broke the connection and dialed Brooke's cell phone, it rang three times and then she answered.

"Hello." By the tone of her voice I knew that I had called at an inopportune time.

"Brooke, this is Gilbert Clancy, I am very sorry to bother you." I heard some muffled speech and then Brooke returned to the phone.

"Hello Mr. Clancy, I needed to step away. Mom must have given you my number. What can I do for you?" she asked, her tone sounding almost relieved. Perhaps her date was not meeting her expectations.

"Brooke, I know the school dance ended at eleven o'clock. Did you and Caitlin go anywhere afterwards; a party or a restaurant?" I asked.

"Yes, we did stop by Toby Hillerman's house. He had a party," Brooke said.

"Were you and Caitlin together the whole evening? Did you eat or drink anything there?"

"There wasn't much food, but there was a lot of beer and alcohol. I didn't drink anything; my mom is really strict about that. Caitlin was drinking a lot and she asked me to drive home. I know she planned to have a bottle of vodka in the car, she usually adds it to her lemonade. I'm pretty sure she didn't drink any of it." Brooke explained. I could tell by her tone that she needed to end the call and get back to whatever she'd been doing.

"Do you recall if the vodka bottle was new or had it been opened?" I asked.

"Caitlin never took a new bottle. Her parents always keep their liquor in those fancy crystal decanters. She always helped herself to what was left." She paused. "Mr. Clancy, is there anything else? I really need to get back to my date."

"No, nothing else Brooke and thanks again." The connection broke and I found myself wondering if we had a completely different crime scene. Could I be wrong? Was Caitlin the unfortunate victim of poison intended for one of her parents? Did someone add poison to the vodka bottle instead?

I reached for my phone and fumbled with the contact directory. One would think that I'd have the number programmed.

"Hi Gil, how do?" Bobby asked in his usual upbeat tone.

"Bobby do you still have Caitlin's car in the impound lot?" I asked rushing past Sylvia and reaching for my car keys.

"Yes we do, why?"

"Did you find a bottle of vodka in it?" I asked.

"Honey, I'll be right back," I said to Sylvia over the phone and ran out the door.

"Yes."

"Did you check it for poison and fingerprints?"

"We dusted it for fingerprints. We found the girl's and her parent's. We didn't test it for poison. I'm on it now," Bobby said. I could hear noises in the background that told me he was rushing through the station.

"I'm on my way, can I see the car?" I asked

"Yes, I'll have it pulled into the garage," Bobby said. I heard him lower the phone and in the background I could hear him talking. "Hey Joe, would you bring the O'Brien car into the garage? Gilbert Clancy is on his way over and would like to see it."

"Got it," I heard Joe say.

"Gil, it will be ready when you get here."

CHAPTER SIXTEEN

ONE POISON TOO MANY

At seven thirty I pulled into the back lot of the Milford Police station, Bobby was waiting for me at the garage door. As I walked up, I noticed that he was still wearing his shirt and tie. How many hours did he work today? How many hours had he worked this week? He didn't seem to have much of a life outside of his job.

"Good call on the vodka bottle Gil," Bobby said and extended his hand as I got closer. "Either we hadn't thought of it, or it's time to get some new forensic techs. They seem to be watching too much CSI and missed the Purloined Letter. A lemonade cup with the girl's finger prints was found on the floor of the car. Both have been sent to the lab, we should have the results back in the morning."

"I spoke to Brooke and she mentioned that Caitlin had a bottle in the car," I said as we stepped through the door into the Police Garage. Caitlin's silver Cobalt sat under focused bright lights.

"Chevrolet Cobalt SS," Bobby said as we crossed the garage, "silver, six speed manual transmission, and a 260 horsepower turbocharged engine. It's about time they came out with something like this. The Japanese have been kicking our ass's way too long. I'm thinking of getting one myself."

"What about the police car?" I asked.

"Like I said, I am thinking about getting one of these for myself." From Bobby's expression, his "company car" was getting old.

We stood as men often do, admiring the car. The aggressive styling was accented with low profile polished aluminum wheels and a large spoiler on the deck lid. I could have done without that particular option, but Bobby was right it was excellent small car.

"Very nice car and lots of power, had her foot remained on the accelerator we might have had some casualties," Bobby said.

I was more concerned about its proximity to Sylvia's store. I pulled the passenger door open and began to look inside. The vehicle's left side; hood, fender, and door were damaged and then forced open by firefighters during the post accident rescue. The windows were closed and the contents remained dry and untouched, except for the efforts of the forensic techs.

Compact Disks lay strewn about the seats and on the floor. Blood and vomit stained the driver's and passenger seats. White air bags that would have saved Caitlin hung lifeless from the steering column and instrument panel.

"Where was the vodka bottle?" I asked Bobby as he stood watching from outside the open passenger's door.

"It was under the passenger's seat."

"How much was left in it?"

"About four ounces, more than enough for a few drinks. I understand from my own discussions with Ms. Kincade that she did not partake in the post dance drinking. A very smart decision," Bobby said as his phone rang and he stepped away from the car.

I could hear Bobby's muffled uh hun, uh hun as he made notes in a small notepad. It was when I heard him say more sternly, "please repeat that again," that I stopped searching the car and turned too looked back at him. The look he returned said we had a problem.

"Please double check your results," Bobby said. I watched his brow furrow. "I don't care how many times you've checked, please check them again. Okay, thanks." Bobby folded his phone shut and looked at me. Then with a nod of his head he gestured for me to follow and we stepped over to a quiet corner of the garage.

"That was the forensic lab. The poison in the cup is the same poison that killed the girl. The poison in the vodka is a cyanide base poison, which means we now have two different poisons and two different crime scenes." Bobby paused for a moment and then went on. "Gil, either we have a murderer who wanted to make sure Caitlin was dead, or we have more than one murderer. Do you believe it's a coincidence that two separate murderers acted independently on the same night to kill the same girl? The game has just changed."

Bobby seemed to draw energy from the new complexities in the case. "Do you think the poison was in the vodka bottle when it left the O'Brien's home, suggesting that it was intended for someone else? Perhaps one of the parents had plans for the other, and it got screwed up when their daughter took the bottle. Maybe Caitlin was a victim by mistake?" Bobby asked.

I'd asked myself the same questions only hours before.

"I don't know Bobby, Mr. O'Brien drinks a very fine Scotch. Perhaps Mrs. O'Brien drinks vodka, which suggests that poison was meant for her." As I said it the list of possible scenario's and suspects increased exponentially.

I put on my cloth gloves and leaned further into the car. The Cobalt was very nice with a finely appointed leather interior and Bose CD player. The foot pedals were upgraded to metal with rubber treads for racing. Not something a girl would want to attempt barefoot, but cool none the less.

I noticed that a key and key fob was still hanging in the ignition. Since the car had stalled and was not running at the scene of the accident, the fireman and forensic techs paid them little notice. "Bobby has your team completed their work on this car?" I asked over my shoulder. When he didn't answer, I turned and found him in spirited discussion with someone on his cell phone.

He lowered the phone from his ear. "Go ahead Gil, we're all done."

I pulled the single key and fob from the ignition. Instinctively I reached into my pocket and pulled out my own keys. I had a set of car keys, a house key, the keys to Sylvia's store, and a key to my office. Why was there only one key on this ring? I flipped the key fob over and saw a raised number two on the back. This was not her regular set of car keys.

"Did you find anything?" Bobby asked leaning into the door opening.

"Look at the car keys on the front seat. The single key and fob came out of the ignition, and the other blob of keys are mine. What gets your attention first?"

"You got way too many keys?' Bobby said.

"Bobby, where are her house keys? Where are the other keys that should be on the ring?" I asked.

"This is her spare key. She was deathly ill and confused and she reached for the first set she could find," Bobby said attempting to explain the situation.

"So that means we can go back to the O'Brien house and they'll have her keys hanging in the rack?" I asked.

"We have her purse we can look and see if the other keys are there. You want to see it?"

"Yes," I said extricating myself from the car.

"Hey Joe would you leave the car here for a while, Gil and I will probably be back to look at it later," Bobby said as we crossed the garage heading back into the actual station.

"Sure Bobby, it'll be here till you tell me to move it," Joe said looking up from his newspaper and Mountain Dew.

I followed Bobby back to his office and took a seat while he went to the storage room to retrieve Caitlin's belongings.

Bobby returned a few minutes later with a plain brown shopping bag. He opened the top, looked inside and compared the contents against an inventory list, then reached in and handed me a very expensive looking purse. It was small, made of fine leather, and closed with a silver buckle emblazoned with the word Coach.

"This has been searched and dusted right?" I asked.

"Yeah, we're all set Gil look at whatever you would like. Just put everything back where you found it. Her personal belongings will be released in a couple of days," Bobby said and turned his attention to other things.

I sat down on the couch and set the purse on the scarred and well worn coffee table. I'd been in Caitlin's home, her bedroom, her locker, and now her car. As I looked at the purse, I feared I would soon know the most intimate secrets of her life. I never entered my wife's purse; instead choosing to hand it to her so she could retrieve what I needed. I opened the chrome buckle and the first thing that drew my attention was the smell of fine perfume. My sense of smell has always been the strongest, and I'm one who will be launched into a favorite memory by a specific smell. My very favorite smell is that of autumn dew and sun-warmed fallen leaves.

I removed the bi-fold wallet and opened it. I found her driver's license, bank card, library card, pictures of her friends, and lots of cash. Caitlin O'Brien it seemed wanted for nothing material.

I set the wallet aside and went on. I found lipstick, a small tube of hand lotion, hairbrush, her cell phone, and to my disappointment, her birth control pills. What I did not find was another set of car keys or her house keys. Had she lost them or were they stolen? If they'd been stolen then the killer would have access to her car and the O'Brien home.

My thoughts turned back to the bottle of Grey Goose Vodka, very expensive and obviously from the family's private stores. I wondered if the poison was put in the vodka at home, perhaps by some of Mr. O'Brien's so called "business associates." There still existed a theory that the poison was intended for Pamela O'Brien, who was, after all involved in a bold and open affair that once made public, would ruin the reputation of a well respected member of the community.

"Did you find anything?" Bobby asked as he reentered his office with fresh coffee.

"No, the keys aren't here." I said as I closed the latch on Caitlin's purse, all the contents returned. "That missing set of keys really bothers me. The key in the ignition was her spare. If I can make a suggestion, your folks should go back to the O'Brien's house and test all of their liquor for poison." I thought back to the scotch I'd enjoyed with Mr. O'Brien, thankful that they hadn't picked another liquor to poison.

"I'll send the forensics team there right now," Bobby said as I handed him the evidence bag.

CHAPTER SEVENTEEN

ANTHONY MACHIAVELLI

On Monday morning Sergio pulled up in a Cadillac CTS-V, black and gleaming in the early morning sun.

"Back up?" Sylvia asked as she gestured toward the expensive car in the drive. We walked onto the porch, she kissed me goodbye and then waved to Sergio, who smiled waving back. The passenger window went down and Sergio turned down some classical music in the car.

"Good morning Mrs. Clancy."

"Good Morning Sergio," Sylvia said wearing a mischievous smile. I also noticed that Morgan had come out of the house, book bag in hand and leaving for school a little earlier than usual. What is it about the women in my house?

"Bye, got some studying to do," she said as she descended the stairs and stepped onto the driveway.

Sylvia feigned a surprised look at her watch and then back to our daughter, trying not to laugh at the nonchalant way Morgan stole glances at the handsome Italian driving the black car.

"I'll call you later." I said and then got into the car.

"Sergio thanks for joining me this morning," I said as we pulled out of the driveway and onto the street.

"Mr. Bertini's trust in Mr. Machiavelli has deteriorated in light of the recent events. He asked me to join you and take him that message," he explained as we pulled onto Interstate 96 headed east. Machiavelli's business was located in Troy.

In today's fast-paced society people have become impatient and often push the envelope of safety, and this day was no different. I could tell that Sergio had been trained in defensive driving by the way he held his hands on the steering wheel, and the way his eyes remained focused on the road and traffic around the car. The CTS was smooth, agile, and powerful, giving no indication that we were traveling well in excess of 80 miles per hour.

The volume of the audio system faded and Sergio spoke for the first time since we'd pulled onto the expressway. "Mr. Bertini has updated me on your business with Mr. Machiavelli. It is inexcusable to involve family members, especially children in irreconcilable circumstances. If Mr. Machiavelli has violated this most basic of rules, he will not be in business long. When a wrong has been committed and trust in an associate compromised, compensation must be paid to the injured party, and if an amicable relationship cannot go on then all parties simply walk away. If resolution cannot be reached, level headed businessmen seek out a mediator. Mr. Bertini would have gladly taken on that role between Mr. O'Brien and Mr. Machiavelli."

I know that Salvatore had taught his employees the value of fair play and the use of a tactical retreat when required, so I felt that level heads would prevail in our meeting with Machiavelli. The balance of our trip was spent in discussion about our families. Sergio was married to a beautiful woman from the island of Malta. Her name was Maria and their union so far had been blessed them with two beautiful children.

The trip had taken no more than thirty minutes and we pulled into the parking lot of European Mold and Manufacturing. Sergio got out of the car first. I noted how quickly his trained eye assessed the parking lot and surrounding buildings. He was impeccably dressed for the meeting in pressed khaki slacks and a crisp white oxford shirt, open at the collar. His oxblood loafers looked freshly polished. He opened the rear passenger door, removed a lightweight sports coat from a hanger, and then joined me at the back of the car. Together we walked into the building.

When we entered the marble and cherry wood lobby of European Mold and Manufacturing, a well dressed woman stood as we approached the desk. "Good morning gentlemen, you must be Mr. Clancy and Mr. Faggini. Please sign our guest register and I will escort you to Mr. Machiavelli's office." The receptionist's name was Susan. She rounded her desk, unlocked the glass security doors, and joined us in the corridor. It was a short walk to the conference room where we would meet with Machiavelli.

She smiled at Sergio, knocked, and then opened the door. "Here you are gentlemen."

A powerful looking man in an expensive suit stood to greet us as we entered. Rising from their seats around a long conference room table, three of Machiavelli's "sales reps" stood, their attention focused on Sergio, who remained a step behind me.

"Mr. Clancy, good morning," Machiavelli said as he offered his hand. His grip was strong from many years of hard work.

"Good morning Mr. Machiavelli and thank you for taking the time to see us this morning." With my greeting done, I stepped aside and Sergio stepped forward.

"Good morning Sergio," Machiavelli said and extended his hand.

"Good morning Mr. Machiavelli. Mr. Bertini sends his regards."

"Gentlemen, please join us." Machiavelli offered us seats at the long table and motioned for one of his assistants to bring us coffee.

With coffee served, Machiavelli looked to his employees gathered around the table. "Gentlemen, if you'll excuse us for a few minutes." I watched the others leave and when the door closed Machiavelli spoke.

"Mr. Clancy, what can I do for you this morning?" he asked, leaning back slightly in his chair at the end of the table. From the large CAD computer screen on the wall, it was obvious they were conducting business before our arrival.

"Mr. Machiavelli as you know Caitlin O'Brien died last week of questionable causes. I have been asked to conduct an informal investigation," I said.

"Jacob O'Brien and I have been friends and business associates for some time. Jacob's confidence and faith in our products and services has helped us build this," Machiavelli said gesturing to the conference room around them.

"Mr. Machiavelli, I had an interview with Mr. O'Brien and he told me of your generous gifts, including the land where his home now sits. He also told me that as of late he's felt pressured by your requests to keep contract work coming to your company." I could see from his expression that Machiavelli didn't like what he heard, and that he was very uncomfortable with the idea that a perfect stranger knew so much of his business practices.

"Mr. O'Brien also told me about threats to himself and his family. He also believes that you had something to do with his daughter's recent death." I watched Machiavelli's lips tighten, either from anger or from Jacob O'Brien's betrayal. I chose my next words carefully. "I am here to ask you Mr. Machiavelli, do you know anything about the death of Caitlin O'Brien?" I knew that I had clearly stepped over the line and very soon I would be dealt with. I waited for the hammer to fall.

Machiavelli sat quietly and said nothing. His eyes were locked on mine, and I was certain that he was considering his next words very carefully. Then he leaned forward, interlocked his fingers and placed his powerful hands gently on the table. Good guy or bad, there is an unwritten rule that someone of Mr. Machiavelli's standing is never to be spoken too in the manner that I had just done.

"Mr. Clancy," Machiavelli began, "as I mentioned earlier Jacob O'Brien is a very good friend of mine. The death of his daughter is a tragedy, and my heart breaks as I think of the pain that he and Pamela must be going through. Our mutual friend Salvatore Bertini and I live by a very strict code of honor in life and in business. If threats were made against Jacob O'Brien, they did not come from me. If they came from one of my employees, I promise they will be dealt with accordingly."

Then he paused for a moment before continuing. "Mr. Clancy, through Jacob I came to know Caitlin very well, and the news of her death was as much a shock to me as it was to her family. All I know is what you have shared with me today. With that knowledge I can promise you this. I will find out who did this unspeakable act, and when I do they will pay for their actions."

Then Machiavelli turned to Sergio. "Sergio, please reassure Salvatore that I would never conduct my business affairs in this manner, and let him know that we are at his service."

"I will Mr. Machiavelli. Mr. Bertini would also like you to know that his friendship and faith in you is unwavering."

The meeting was now over. I stood and extended my hand to Mr. Machiavelli sure that I had just made a very deadly enemy. "Mr. Machiavelli, please forgive me for bringing your honor and integrity into question. Thank you for seeing us this morning," I said.

Machiavelli stood still, firmly gripping my hand. "Mr. Clancy, I respect your honesty, your dedication to the truth, and your courage. There are not many men who would have confronted me with such a direct question."

I tried to put a brave face on, but I'm sure he noted my ashen tone and the slight shimmer of sweat on my brow.

"Mr. Clancy you leave here as a friend. If Jacob feels uncomfortable with our business relationship I will dissolve it immediately. In our eagerness to provide our customers with the best service, we may have gotten a little overzealous. Now if you will please excuse me, I have another meeting."

"Thank you Mr. Machiavelli," I said.

Machiavelli shook Sergio's hand and we filed out of the conference room. Susan was waiting for us in the hall and soon we were walking to the car.

Once inside the car and on our way home I looked to Sergio. "Did I push him too far? I meant to extend Mr. Machiavelli the respect due to a man in his position, but that particular line of questioning must be direct and to the point."

"Mr. Clancy you've earned Mr. Bertini's respect and trust because of your dedication to the truth. This pursuit requires clear and direct questions that leave no ambiguity in the mind of those you address. You did well, men like Mr. Machiavelli do not offer their hand in friendship to those who have angered or offended them."

Thirty minutes later I thanked Sergio for the escort and then watched him drive away from the house. I trusted Machiavelli in the same way I've always trusted Sal Bertini. Both are men who conduct their lives and run their businesses with honor and an iron fist. They are dangerous men to be celebrated, respected, and feared. Machiavelli was a puzzle piece that did not belong. I felt that Jacob O'Brien had just sent me on a wild goose chase.

CHAPTER EIGHTEEN

BETTY MCINTYRE

I picked up lunch and surprised Sylvia, who was quietly working when I opened the door and stepped inside. My wife looked over the top her of glasses and smiled. I couldn't be sure if it was a smile for me, or one for the bags of deli food that I held in each hand.

"Perfect timing," she said as she rose from her seat and kissed my cheek. It still gave me butterflies in my stomach.

"I wanted to let you know that Sergio and I left our meeting with Machiavelli safe and sound," I said, handing Sylvia her favorite sandwich; tuna fish on tomato basil bread.

"Morgan will be pleased to know that her father has survived another day. So how did your meeting with the infamous Mr. Machiavelli go?" she asked, wiping her mouth with a napkin and sipping her iced tea.

"Machiavelli is everything his namesake would suggest. He's rich, very powerful, intelligent, feared and respected," I told her.

"Basically the perfect man," Sylvia said before taking another bite of her sandwich.

"My love, he is a bit older than you and quite scary," I told her.

"I'd have him purring like a big tom cat," she said and then laughed wickedly.

"Are you finished?" I asked.

"Yes dear," she said.

"Machiavelli is not involved in this. He most likely learned of Caitlin's death from Sal Bertini. O'Brien's claim that he was threatened by Machiavelli or a member of his team is a lie. Machiavelli also assured me that if the business relationship between himself and O'Brien has become strained, he would immediately dissolve it."

"What's next?" Sylvia asked.

"I guess I'll head back up to the high school. I need to learn more about Jonathon Peters, which also seems to be another loose end to clean up." The truth be told, I didn't know what was next, and with that we finished our lunch.

At one thirty I stopped by Executive Offices and picked up the personnel file for Jonathon Peters from Mrs. Busch, who greeted me with her usual scowl.

"Good Afternoon Mrs. Busch," I said and gave her my best smile. Most women eventually succumbed to my charms, but this one had a cast iron constitution. She frowned, and without a word handed me a large manila envelope with my name on it.

"Thank you," I said and crossed the cul-de-sac to the office of Bartimus Brunt, Dean of Students.

"Gilbert, get in here man!" Bartimus was up from his chair and on me in an instant. This was no easy task considering that over the last twenty five years since our college days, Barti as we had called him in school had gone to seed. "Baker said you were here investigating the O'Brien death. How are things going?" he asked.

I met Barti in third grade at Baker Elementary. His family came from England when his dad went to work for General Motors. I could remember his accent being so strong that no one, including the teachers could understand him. I seemed to be the first to break the language barrier and our friendship blossomed from there. After a rocky start he persevered and became a scholar in math and science. He could have gone to college anywhere in the country but chose to join me and Sylvia at Eastern Michigan, where he earned his degree in Secondary Education. Eventually he found his way into administration and has become the finest Dean of Students in the district.

"Things are going," I said with a slight shrug. "Somewhat of a slow process, fitting the pieces together that belong, and throwing the others away."

Barti reached across his desk and handed me another manila envelope. "This is the information you requested. They are copies so please shred them when you are done."

"Thanks Barti." I patted my old friend on one his broad shoulders.

"Good luck."

"Thanks."

I returned to the library at one forty five and found Brooke Kincaid waiting outside my conference room door.

"Good afternoon Brooke."

"Hi Mr. Clancy, how's it going?"

"Fine, come in." I hadn't been there in a few days and the conference room smelled like it had been closed up. I stepped over to a window and pushed open the pane of glass. "Ah, that's better." Then I turned to Brooke Kincade, who had taken a seat at the round interview table, her look was one of concern.

"Brooke, you are probably wondering why we have spoken so often these last few days?" I asked, while adding carefully measured scoops of coffee into a filter.

"Well," she paused, "actually I have. Mr. Clancy, you don't suspect me of anything do you?"

"Of course not, but you were with Caitlin before she died. You knew more about her than anyone else. Your information is helping to solve this mystery." She smiled and I could see the tension fading.

"I need to ask you a few more questions, and then I know you need to get out of here, so I'll make it fast. By the way you ran an excellent two mile against Lakeland last week."

"Thanks," Brooke said and then smiled. She was an outstanding runner and bound for a scholarship if she stayed healthy.

"Brooke, do you know if Caitlin lost a set of keys for the new car?"

Brooke looked at me totally surprised. "How did you know that?" she asked. "Yes, she did lose her keys. We were sitting in the library, right over by that window." She pointed to a table that was surrounded by bookshelves, and faced a large window that overlooked the football field. "We got up to leave and she couldn't find her keys. We searched everywhere and they were gone. I drove her home to get her spare and brought her back to get her car before her mom found out."

"Thanks Brooke, the missing car keys have been bothering me for some time." The coffee finished brewing and I poured a cup. I offered Brooke some coffee, but she declined with a wrinkled nose and a quick shake of her head.

"How is your investigation going?" She asked.

"I'm getting closer every day. Good luck this afternoon," I said as she rose from her seat and turned to leave.

"Thanks."

As Brooke left Mrs. Fortier entered the conference room. "How are you Mr. Clancy?"

"I am doing fine Monique, and please call me Gil. Would you like some coffee? I just made it."

"Yes I would, thank you." Monique Fortier sat down at the round table. I handed her a cup of coffee and then sat down.

"How is your investigation going?" she asked between sips.

"Slow," I said surprised at her sudden arrival and inquiry.

"Please let me know if there is anything I can do to help. I'm quite good at doing research, and I do have some slow times during the day."

"I will, and thank you," I said as Monique Fortier rose from her seat, coffee cup in hand and left my office. I watched her leave, wondered why she had just volunteered to help with the investigation.

I opened the manila envelope and removed Jonathon Peters' resume and a copy of his application to the school district. Peters also graduated from Eastern Michigan with a degree in Art, and

Secondary Education with a concentration in Communication and Theatre Arts. Later he earned a Masters Degree in Visual Art. He began his teaching career at Miamisburg Middle School, in Miamisburg, Ohio. He worked there from September, 1980 through June, 1984.

The school's principal at the time of his employment was a woman named Betty McIntyre, whom I would call her before leaving today. In September of 1984 Peters hired into Milford High School as an Art Teacher and from all reports, remained in that position until the investigation and his eventual dismissal in 2008.

Peter's time in Ohio ended almost twenty five years ago, but it was worth a try. I found the number for Miamisburg Middle School and the hunt for Ms. Betty McIntyre was on.

"Miamisburg Middle School may I help you?" The cheery voice answered. I was certain she was one of the army of volunteers so critical to the survival of our schools. Thanks go out to all the volunteers!

"Good afternoon, my name is Gilbert Clancy and I'm looking for a Ms. Betty McIntyre."

"One moment please." The phone went to hold and I thought just how well my day was going when a woman answered.

"This is Betty McIntyre, how can I help you?"

CHAPTER NINETEEN

NATHAN EDMUNDS

"Ms. McIntyre, my name is Gilbert Clancy. If you have a moment may I have a word about a former employee of yours named Jonathon Peters."

"Mr. Clancy will you hold for one moment please," she said and set the phone down. I could hear muffled voices in the background and assumed she was finishing her business or excusing someone from her office. I heard the door close and she picked up the phone.

"Mr. Clancy, how can I help you?" she asked.

I told her of Caitlin's death, my involvement as an unofficial investigator, and Caitlin's complaint against Peters two years before.

"Jonathon Peters was a great teacher. He started out as a Physical Education teacher, then we moved him to regular classroom instruction, and then to the Art department. He was a very talented artist," Ms. McIntyre explained.

I noted that her tone began to lose some of its fervor as her review of Peters continued. I could tell that something was wrong.

"Ms. McIntyre why was Jonathon Peters moved around so

much, were you looking to build his experience? Was he identified as a candidate for future leadership?" I asked.

"Actually, we were trying to find the right position for Mr. Peters," Ms. McIntyre said with a bit of shame and regret in her voice. "You see Mr. Clancy, Jonathon Peters seemed to like the children a bit too much. This made some of the students very uncomfortable, and their parents furious. Accusations were made and eventually he was let go. I encouraged him to seek another line of work. When he left, he took our school's nurse with him and I've been told that they later wed." She paused. "From what you are telling me, Jonathon remained an educator and further issues ensued."

"Yes, there was the issue with Caitlin O'Brien, but from what I understand his innocence was greatly defended by the school's principal. She stood by him until the school board forced him out. You mentioned the school nurse. What was her name," I asked.

"Monique Boudreaux."

When she said it I turned to the library's reference desk and the only Monique I'd ever met. She turned as if sensing my look and smiled back. I wondered for an instance if she could hear my conversation.

"Mr. Clancy, are you still there?" Betty McIntyre's voice brought me back to the moment.

"Ms. McIntyre, I do have one more question. Did any students die during Jonathon Peters' tenure at your school?" I was getting very good and now very comfortable with asking the tough questions.

"Yes we did," she said and then paused for a moment. "Mr. Clancy, I've been a middle school Principal for over forty years. I've supervised thousands of students and lost only one. It is almost beyond coincidence that you should ask me that question. The boy's name was Nathan Edmunds; he was a seventh grader and one of Jonathan's students. He complained about some of the things Jonathan said, and some of the physical contact that had gone on in class.

The boy's parents came to the school and demanded an

apology. This of course was years before any action was ever taken against the teacher or complaints made public. We made the formal apologies and I moved Jonathon from physical education into a regular classroom. A couple of weeks later, Nathan, who had an allergy to peanuts, mistakenly ate food containing peanut oil. His reaction was immediate and he died when the swelling in his throat restricted his ability to breath. It was the very worst day of my life." She stopped talking and I felt very bad that I'd made her relive such a terrible moment in her life.

"Ms. McIntyre, thank you for the information and I'm sorry to make you revisit such bad memories. I do have a favor to ask."

"Go ahead Mr. Clancy."

"Ms. McIntyre, may I come down to your school tomorrow and review whatever information you may have on Peters and Boudreaux? I think there may be a connection between what happened there and our death in Michigan."

"Of course Mr. Clancy, I'll have that information ready when you arrive. I'll see you tomorrow." Betty McIntyre broke the connection. I set the phone down and leaned back in my chair.

I watched Monique Fortier at her desk helping the students. Smiling and laughing, she seemed to really enjoy her work. Was she Monique Boudreaux, who twenty five years ago was in another school when another student died? I was on a roll, so I thought I would call Mrs. Busch.

"Mrs. Busch, I need to get a copy of Monique Fortier's resume. My request is confidential and would you meet me in the school's main lobby?"

"Yes Mr. Clancy, I will have that for you right away." I heard the phone connection break and I realized that some people react to things differently. It was obvious that Mrs. Busch was all business and didn't respond to my sucking up. I would note that for later requests.

I had to restrain myself from running. A deadly pattern was beginning to emerge; two dead children, very similar circumstances, and possibly the same two adults. How many other children had died of suspicious causes in their past? Mrs. Busch

117

was standing in the main lobby with a manila envelope in her hand.

"Per your request Mr. Clancy, let me know if you need anything else." Then to my surprise, she smiled.

"Thank you Mrs. Busch." I smiled, patted her shoulder, and then headed back to the library. In an empty corridor I stopped and opened the envelope, and read the document. According to her resume Monique had been employed at Miamisburg Middle School, so there is no doubt she was the school nurse at the time of Peters' employment. I also noted that Monique Fortier had changed jobs frequently, was this due to incompetence or were there other reasons? I would need Bobby's help to investigate all of her previous employers. What I really wanted to know was how long she'd been married to, and more important, how long had she been divorced from Peters? Why would she kill now? Peters had been dead for almost two years.

This and a thousand other questions raced through my mind as I packed up my laptop, locked the door to my office, and hurried out. I needed some think time with Sylvia; she'd always been my sanity check when things seemed to be falling into place too quickly.

CHAPTER TWENTY

THE PLOT THICKENS

Really," I heard Bobby say as I struggled with the house keys, my cell phone, and computer bag.

"Yes, before Peters came to Michigan, he lived and taught school in Ohio. Monique Boudreaux, whom we know to be Monique Fortier, left with him."

"She has a daughter named Emmeline. Is she Peter's daughter?" Bobby asked.

"I'm checking on that now," I said.

"Alright, let me know what you find out." Bobby broke the connection and the line went silent.

I had just set my things down when Sylvia appeared at the top of the basement stairs. "Hello," I said.

"Hello my dear." She came forward, kissed my cheek, and allowed me to take her in my arms.

"What were you doing downstairs, is something broken?" I asked.

"No, I was just looking at the pictures from the dance again hoping something might catch my eye or look out of place," Sylvia said.

"Did anything look out of place?" I asked.

"No, but I can't help wondering about the mystery hand. I'd feel a whole lot better if we knew who she was. Let me look into that," Sylvia said and pulled my hand away from her lower back before it slid down any further, and led me into the kitchen. "Come on, dinner's ready."

I explained what I'd discovered so far and then broke the news. "I need to drive to Miamisburg, Ohio tomorrow morning. I need to get a better understanding of Jonathan Peters, Monique Fortier, and the accidental death of a boy named Nathan Edwards." I could tell that Sylvia wasn't happy, but she seemed to soften when I mentioned the death of another child.

"How long will you be gone?" she asked. Though she tried to hide it I could still hear a bit of frustration in her voice.

"I'll leave at four thirty tomorrow morning. I am scheduled to meet with a Ms. Betty McIntyre; Principal of the town's Middle School, and the former boss of Peters and Fortier. I'll be home for dinner," I said trying to ease the tension. We both understood how important this investigation was, but it didn't hide the fact that it created undue stress on our family.

After dinner, with the dishes done and Morgan now settled in her room to work on many hours of homework, Sylvia and I sat at the kitchen table and I told her everything I knew. "I thought Caitlin's case against Peters might have something to do with her death, and with nothing else to go on, I began to look into Peters' past. He began his career in a small town called Miamisburg. Guess who else was there?" I asked.

"Don't know," Sylvia replied as she glanced at the newspaper.

"Monique Fortier, whose maiden name was Monique Boudreaux before she married Jonathon Peters, and if I'm not mistaken, Emmeline Fortier is Peters' daughter, which would certainly explain her bitterness toward Caitlin. First she has to endure the public humiliation of her father's investigation, dismissal, and death, and then the loss of the School's Scholarship to the same girl."

"I can understand her frustration. Depending upon her state of mind, it could be motive enough to kill. She may have just snapped," Sylvia suggested her mind racing through the possible scenarios. "But before we go too far down that line of thought, you need to read this."

She slid the paper to me. It was opened to the announcements.

At the top of the column was Emmeline Fortier's senior picture. Below it the announcement said.

Mr. and Mrs. Victor Fortier are pleased to announce that their daughter, Emmeline has been awarded a full academic scholarship to Michigan State University. Ms. Fortier will study Pre-Med with plans to go onto the University's School of Medicine.

I reread the announcement a second time and then looked back at Sylvia who shrugged her shoulders.

"Where does that leave your theory now?" She asked.

"Emmeline is still a suspect. Public humiliation at the hand of someone like Caitlin O'Brien seems a pretty tough pill to swallow." I opened my computer bag and pulled out the envelope that Barti had given me.

"Barti sends his regards by the way." I wasn't sure I liked the way Sylvia's face brightened up at the mention of the name.

"How is Barti?" she asked.

"Barti's fine, but I am concerned at the way your face seems to light up at the mention of his name. You don't still fancy him do you?" I asked without looking up from the stack of papers I was going through.

"Barti's just cute and you know it," she said trying to dodge my question.

The word "cute" was not the first word that came to mind when I thought of Bartimus Brunt, but then again my lovely wife thinks frogs and toads are also cute. I took pleasure from that thought and then returned to the business of the mystery at hand. The packet I'd gotten from Barti contained Emmeline Fortier's school records since her kindergarten years. Her name had been Emmeline Peters through second grade. In third grade she returned to school as Emmeline Fortier having been adopted by her mother's new husband.

Why such a separation from her father? She never mentioned it in our interview, nor did she mention the humiliation and anger she must have felt towards Caitlin. Did she kill Caitlin because of her father, or because of the school's scholarship, that now she didn't need?

"What are you thinking?" Sylvia asked. She'd gotten up and rounded the table to look over my shoulder, reading the documents in my hand. She lay an arm across my shoulder and put her face close to mine. She was letting me know that I was no longer in the doghouse.

"How did she do it?" I said posing the question to no one in particular. "She most likely knew that Caitlin always drank lemonade. Every cup of lemonade on the table at the dance had a top on it. There was no way she could have guessed which one Caitlin would take, and why take the chance of poisoning the wrong person. To further complicate things, I still cannot figure out how the poison got in the vodka bottle, which did not kill Caitlin? Bobby's forensic team checked all the liquor at the O'Brien's house. None of the other bottles were poisoned, so it wasn't an attempted murder that had gone bad," I said rubbing my forehead in frustration.

"There's still Principal Baker, whom I've not taken off my list yet. Caitlin had messages from him in her locker and on her tablet. Even though the affair with her mother was no secret, I am sure that Caitlin used that information to her advantage. She may have chosen the wrong person to cross," I said as Sylvia retook her seat and glanced back down at the paper.

"I cannot place him on the security tapes entering the building, nor does he appear in any of the photos at the dance. The only proof that Principle Baker was even in the building was at the end of the night, seeing the kids out after the dance. I didn't see Monique Fortier enter the building, but I did see her in a few photos, and then again at the end of the dance. Had both chosen to work late and then help out at the dance?"

"Perhaps there is something going on between Baker and Fortier," Sylvia suggested. "I've seen her and she is a very beautiful woman. They both seem to be looking for something more, if you know what I mean." Sylvia completed her thought with raised eyebrows, suggesting that the something between Baker and Fortier might be a naughty something.

"And the plot thickens," I said between sips of coffee.

Sylvia got up and put her coffee cup in the sink, and then she leaned down and kissed my cheek. "The puzzle always goes together one piece at a time and every piece has to fit. Don't stay up too late." Then with a wink she drifted from the kitchen. Mr. Jones followed close behind.

CHAPTER TWENTY ONE

MIAMISBURG

The building's tan brick and aluminum framed doors reminded me of my own beloved school. I entered the main office and found her standing tall amid the morning's chaos, unflustered by the activity. When I met the eye of Betty McIntyre she smiled and motioned for me to follow. A moment later we stood in the quiet of her office.

"Mr. Clancy," she smiled and extended her hand in greeting.

"It is a pleasure and please call me Gilbert," I said as we walked through her office into an adjoining conference room. The long table was well organized with neatly stacked school reports, yearbooks, and information that I was sure pertained to the time when Peters and Fortier walked the halls of this fine institution of learning.

"You've been busy Ms. McIntyre," I said wondering just how many hours she'd spent collecting and then organizing this information given the fact that only fourteen had passed since we last spoke.

She smiled for a moment, "Gilbert, I would prefer you call me Betty." Then just as quickly anger stole her smile, she turned and quietly faced a large window that looked out over the school grounds. She spoke without turning to face me. "The death of any child is a tragedy. After Nathan died, I questioned my own ability to lead, and my ability to protect my kids. It angers me that another life was lost, and the same two people may somehow be part of it. I spent the greater part of last night doing some of my own research. What you see here is everything I could find relating to the time that Mr. Peters and Ms. Boudreaux were at my school."

Ms. McIntyre showed unforgettable pride when she referred to the building in which we stood as "her" school.

"Betty this is more than I could have asked for, thank you," I said bowing my head respectfully to a woman who had dedicated her life to educating children.

"Please take your time and review everything," Betty said patting my arm gently. Then she gestured to someone in her office and a tall willowy girl entered the room. "Julie will be at your beckoned call. She is a student assistant and free labor so we like to keep her busy," she said and placed a loving hand on the girl's shoulder. Julie looked back at me with a tight lipped slightly embarrassed smile, rolling her eyes. I could tell she was one step away from the finger down the throat, fake vomiting gesture.

"I'll do my best," I promised Betty and then smiled at Julie.

Ms. McIntyre left the room, I started to survey the table and Julie took a seat at a nearby desk. She began to pull books out of an already overstuffed backpack.

"Julie the only thing I really need is a telephone book of the surrounding area, and then you can get back to your homework." I could see the relief in her eyes as she rushed out of the room returning a few minutes later with a stack of bright yellow phone books.

"Thanks Julie, if I need anything else I'll come and find you."

"Alright Mr. Clancy." Then quick as a wink, she was gone.

I picked up the 1980 Miamisburg Vikings yearbook and leafed through the pages until I found the staff photos and a smiling Jonathon Peters. Listed below his picture were his subjects; Physical Education, English, and Art Studies. Peters was very handsome and appeared in many of the yearbook photos. I saw

Peters in his art class; teaching his students to work with jewelry, clay, and paints. Another showed him on a stage, script in hand and directing what appeared to be a musical. Perhaps a bit much for middle school, but you had to appreciate his energy and drive. The final picture showed him dancing with Ms. Elinor McGee, who like Peters appeared to be a new faculty member at the school. The background of the picture showed they were attending the school's Christmas Dance.

Ms. McIntyre had been thorough and left me a list of the current faculty and the 2010 yearbook. Elinor McGee was still a member of the staff. I wanted to talk with her about Peters, from the earlier picture they appeared to have been more than just friends.

I called Julie back into the room and asked her to search the phone books for the name Boudreaux. I returned to the yearbooks and found Monique in the 1982 edition. She'd taken the position as School Nurse after graduating from Ohio State University. She had dark hair and dark eyes, which were no doubt from her French heritage. The resemblance to her now teenage daughter was uncanny. In the photo she chose to wear surgical scrubs instead of the traditional white nurse's uniform. She had a stethoscope around her neck and wore her dark hair feathered, a very popular style at the time.

Next to the stack of yearbooks lay a pile of folders. Upon closer inspection, I found they were the personnel folders on Peters and Boudreaux. I took from Monique's pile first. Based on my earlier discussion with Betty McIntyre, I already knew Peters' work history. Monique joined the staff in September of 1981, and received excellent reviews in 1982 and 1983. 1984 was a much different story. She'd received a number of warnings about being away from the school's medical office for long periods of time.

I read a lengthy entry dated May 31, 1984.

Ms Boudreaux has completely failed in her duties as school's medical nurse. Nathan Edmunds became violently ill from an allergic reaction to peanut oil. Ms. Boudreaux was not in the medical office, nor could she be located. Nathan collapsed and then slipped into an unconscious state. The fire department paramedics were dispatched and could not revive Nathan after repeated injections of steroids. He was later pronounced dead at the hospital.

Ms. Boudreaux is responsible to know the special medical needs of all high risk students. Her actions on this day border on criminal. It should be noted that Ms. Boudreaux was found with Mr. Peters, who was accused of having inappropriate contact with Nathan Edmunds. As of this day, Ms. Boudreaux is terminated from the employment of this school and district.

Ms. Betty McIntyre
Principal, Miamisburg Middle School

How convenient I thought. Did she knowingly allow the school district to use peanut oil in the food being served to the children, or did she slip something into Nathan's food and then disappeared from her post at the most inopportune of times. Did she take vengeance upon the boy who had issued a career ending complaint against the man she loved?

I wrote down her address of record at the time, which was in Springfield, a town just south of Miamisburg. Only one phonebook remained of the stack that Julie had brought earlier, a chartreuse sticky note marked the results of her search. I opened the book to find a Ms. Diana Boudreaux 19250 route 1A, Springfield. The home of Monique's mother would be my last stop of the day before heading north and back home.

I would not solve the murder of Nathan Edmunds today, but I would be back to put things right once the case in Michigan was in order. It was clear that Monique was capable of killing and must be considered a suspect in the murder of Caitlin O'Brien. In 1984 a young boy died because he threatened to tarnish the reputation of the man she loved. Had she killed again more than thirty years later? Was she seeking revenge for Peters whom she had long since divorced, or was there someone else? That question would have to wait as Betty McIntyre wandered back into the conference room.

"Gilbert, I hope this information was helpful. Julie tells me that you have a few more questions."

"Yes I do, but before we go on please let me thank you again. The information you have provided has helped immensely with my investigation. I also want you to know that Julie was an excellent assistant." I looked to Julie who smiled and shook her head at Ms. McIntyre.

"Julie if you don't mind, I would like to speak with Ms. McIntyre privately." Almost before I could finish Julie had already picked up her things, and was hurrying from the conference room.

"Thanks again," I said.

"You're welcome, Mr. Clancy. Have a safe trip home." As the door closed I turned to Betty McIntyre, who had taken a seat at the table.

"Betty, how long did the relationship between Peters and Boudreaux gone on before her dismissal?"

"I guess I really didn't notice anything until after Christmas in nineteen eighty three. Jonathan was engaged to Elinor McGee, who was his college sweetheart. I didn't know of their relationship when they hired in. I had plans to move one of them to another school. They were both very good teachers. That happily ever after was cut short once Monique set her sights on Jonathon."

"He broke the engagement with Ms. McGee and left with Monique?" I asked.

"Yes," Betty said.

I shook my head in understanding.

"Well Betty, thank you very much." I extended my hand and Betty accepted. When I drew it back, she held it for a moment longer. Our eyes met and she spoke.

"You have to catch the one who did this."

"Betty, I promise you the person who killed Caitlin O'Brien will not get away with it. Then when I'm done, I'll be back to look into what really happened to Nathan."

Betty smiled, and I helped her to her feet. "Let me help you put these things back into the boxes." I turned back to the table and Betty gently took my forearm.

She smiled and picked up Peters' and Boudreaux's personnel files. "Don't worry about these things; we have Julie to take care of that." She smiled, taking a moment of pleasure from being the boss.

I smiled back. Then Betty slipped her arm through mine and together we left the conference room.

Springfield was only two exits south of Miamisburg, and Route 1A only five miles west of the expressway. What I've always liked about Ohio and Indiana is their rural character. I drove west and the terrain transformed to rolling hills and farms. 19250 Route 1A was a large farm house sitting on the corner of lineless county roads; one continuing west and other turning north along the edge of the property.

The house had a large wraparound porch and steps leading to a well manicured yard. A field stone fireplace rose high above the home's slate tile roof. Beyond the house sat a garage, barn, and storage buildings. All were in immaculate condition. A large garden ran along the northwest side of the property. I could easily identify the rows of corn and tomatoes plants. In a distant corner, I could see the red stalks and green leaves of rhubarb plants growing in a large circular brick planter. Brilliantly colored flowers of all types grew on the south end of the garden. Gladiolas, roses, and carnations were in all stages of growth, some in colorful blooms.

I didn't see anyone on what appeared to be five acres of land. Mrs. Boudreaux would be in her late seventies or maybe her early eighties. By the look of this garden, she was still very active and energetic. With the information I needed, I turned north on Interstate 75 and headed home.

CHAPTER TWENTY TWO

RICHARD BAKER

"Monique, why didn't tell me that you were once married to Jonathon Peters and that Emma is his daughter?" I asked as we walked back to the library conference room with fresh cups of coffee. I watched Monique's smile fade and her face harden.

"That was a long time ago. Jonathon and I divorced when Emma was three. I met Victor a few years later and he adopted my daughter when she was seven. Jonathon never fought the adoption, nor did he fight for his parental rights. He was a weak and pathetic man who cared more about his students than he did for his own little girl. I regret the day I met him." Monique said her voice thick with contempt.

"Tell me how you felt during the initial O'Brien investigation, and then after his death?" I asked as Monique followed me into the conference room, and slumped down on the couch.

"I was embarrassed and hoped that no one knew or would remember that I'd been married to him. My biggest concern was that reporter following the story. I was sure he would eventually drag Emma into it. I spoke with him repeatedly and finally convinced him to leave her out of it." The look in her eyes made me think that reporter was a very lucky man.

"I'm sure you've already met with Betty McIntyre and you know what Jonathan was accused of in Ohio."

"I did, and I find it hard to believe that after twenty five years that issue resurfaced." Then I leaned forward in my chair to make sure I had Monique's full attention. "This is what I think happened. Mr. Peters gave Caitlin a bad grade, or maybe he didn't give her the lead role in one of his plays. She found out about his past and then used it to take her revenge on him. Her parents hired the best lawyers money could buy and he didn't have a chance. She ruined his career and his life, she never felt guilty nor did she feel any remorse."

"So you think Jonathon was innocent?" Monique asked.

"Yes, and once I have solved Caitlin O'Brien's murder; I intend to clear his name."

When I mentioned solving Caitlin's murder, Monique dropped her eyes for the first time in our conversation. She had something to hide.

"Did your daughter know much about, or remember Peters?" I asked.

"She read his name on her birth certificate. She had questions and we talked about Jonathan, but her earliest memories were with Victor," Monique said a softness returning to her face.

"Did she ever ask to meet him, or have contact with her father as she got older?" I asked as the tension in the room settled.

"I never discouraged her from contacting Jonathan, but to this day I don't know if she ever did."

I knew the chilly interview was over when Monique rose from the couch and headed toward the door. Then she stopped and turned to look back at me.

"Is our interview over, or are there other skeletons in my closet that you would like to discuss?" She asked, her face calm and her dark eyes menacing. "Mr. Clancy, two can play at this game. I think I'll begin my own investigation into those dark secrets you keep hidden just below the surface, and then I'll look into those of your wife and your two daughters."

"Are you threatening me Mrs. Fortier?"

"Mr. Clancy, I don't make threats."

Then with a smile on her face, Monique left the conference room. I knew at moment, I had just made a mortal enemy.

"Mr. Clancy, do you have a moment?"

I looked up from my computer as Richard Baker stepped into the conference room and pulled the door closed behind him.

"Principal Baker, I thought I might be hearing from you today please have a seat," I said gesturing to one of my visitor chairs.

He took a seat and I joined him at the interview table. Once I was seated, he began.

"Gilbert it has come to my attention that your investigation into Caitlin O'Brien's untimely death has taken you into the private lives of some of my staff. Do you think that is really necessary?"

"Are you referring to my earlier discussion with Mrs. Fortier?" I asked.

"Yes, Monique is very uncomfortable with your line of questioning,"

"Principal Baker, as you know this is a murder investigation. Caitlin O'Brien was poisoned in this school, and I don't care who is uncomfortable with my line of questioning," I said, my voice getting louder.

"What led your investigation to Mrs. Fortier?" Baker asked leaning back in his chair, a concerned look on his face.

"I began investigating a possible link between Peters' dismissal and Caitlin's death. I spoke with one of Peters' previous employers, and during that discussion I found out that Monique Fortier, then Monique Boudreaux, worked at the same middle school. After she was terminated for incompetence, they left and came to Michigan when he got a job here."

"Mr. Clancy, I still don't see what that has to do with Caitlin O'Brien's death." Baker said, comfortable that he had just poked another hole in my investigation.

"It's most likely nothing, but a young boy died from unusual circumstances when Peters and Fortier were at that school. Then Caitlin dies at this school and the same two people are around." I said, and then looked at the smug expression on Baker's face. "Principal Baker, I glad you stopped by because I do have a few questions for you."

Baker shifted uneasily in his seat and then his eyes settled on mine. We looked at each other for sometime before he finally spoke. "Mr. Clancy, what would you like to know?"

It was one of those moments where you can do what is right, or you can do what is easy. I looked at him with the certainty that my career hung in the balance of this discussion. With doubts that my "get out of jail free" card was going to save me, I began. "Principal Baker, are you having an affair with Pamela O'Brien?"

"Yes, Pam and I have been in a relationship for about a year," Baker said in a matter of fact tone.

"Is that why you were fast tracking Caitlin to the school's scholarship?" My last question had finally pushed the right button.

"What!" Baker snarled and slammed his fist on the table. He leapt out of his chair and towered over me. He was tall, broad shouldered, and in very good shape. I stood, figuring his next move was toward me. Then just as quickly as he angered, he calmed down. "Caitlin O'Brien was an excellent student and earned her candidacy with hard work and service to the school."

"Prove it," I challenged, "I want to personally audit Caitlin's school records and then interview her teachers. I would also like to see the scholarly work that earned her the right to be a candidate for the School's Scholarship. To be quite honest Principal Baker, I'm just not seeing it."

"Mr. Clancy I think that is a bit beyond the scope of your investigation," he said with a slight growl to his tone. "Furthermore, if you are half as good as they say you are the would-be assassin should already be in custody. My personal affairs and those of my staff are off limits." Then to reinforce the threat, Baker purposely took a step toward me. "Is that clear?"

The man obviously had something to hide, and he was using his position to push me around, and I would have none of it. "Principal Baker, how good or bad I may be is irrelevant to this investigation. The killer will be caught, and I will be the one to catch her." Baker's self-satisfied expression changed slightly, but it was just enough. "Yes, it was a woman who killed Caitlin O'Brien and I think you know something about it," I said, now standing toe to toe with Baker, only inches separating us.

"I want you out of my school right now," Baker said as he turned and left the conference room, slamming the door behind him. I watched him walk away, and then momentarily meet Monique's concerned eye as he passed. When he got to the library's main doors he turned back to look at me, his cell phone already to his ear. I was certain within minutes I'd get a call from Jim White.

I walked straight to Monique's reference desk and stood there until she looked up. "Come near my family," I said, "and you will have a hell of a lot more to worry about than Caitlin O'Brien's murder. Do you understand me?"

When she failed to respond, I asked her again. "Do you understand me?" An almost imperceptible nod of her head told me that she did. I'd played my card, upset the apple cart, and now I would wait for the fallout.

CHAPTER TWENTY THREE

SYLVIA

The much anticipated call from Principal White never came, and I returned home with my employment still intact. My "get out of jail free card" is very similar to James Bond's "license to kill," it allows me to push when needed with the full backing of Principal White, the School District, and of course Lieutenant Bobby Thomas.

When I pulled in the drive my daughter waved from the seat of the riding lawnmower and my wife met me at the door.

"Jim White just called, apparently Richard Baker was complaining about your investigation. Jim told him to get over it, and he asked me to tell you to keep up the good work and finish it. I'll take that to mean you're getting close?" Sylvia asked, smiling and eager to know what I was up to. "You know, don't you?"

"I don't know all the details, but my trip to Ohio and Baker's reaction to my questioning suggests I have another suspect; Monique Fortier.

I went on to explain everything I knew and how too many coincidences seemed to point back to Monique; her affair with Peters, the death of Nathan Edmunds, Caitlin's missing car keys, and the rhubarb in her mother's garden.

"There are still too many lose ends," I warned as Sylvia and I walked into the kitchen. "First, why are there two different poisons, one in the lemonade cup and the other in the vodka bottle? Are there two murderers, and was it just a coincidence that they chose the same night to act, or was there a team, perhaps a mother-daughter act?

"Why not use the same poison then?" Sylvia countered. "Why choose a fast acting cyanide-based poison in the vodka?"

"I don't know. What about the mystery hand at the dance?"

"I'm working on that," Sylvia reassured me confidently.

"Based on what you've told me, you suspect the boy in Ohio was eliminated by Monique because he threatened Peters' career and her happily ever after," Sylvia said as she finished making dinner.

I looked at my wife. How did she know those were Betty McIntyre's exact words?

"If that's true, we know that Monique is capable of committing premeditated murder. She could have easily stolen the keys from Caitlin's unattended purse, and that would have given her unrestricted access to the girl's car and the family's home." Without being directly involved, Sylvia had come to the same conclusion that I had, Monique Fortier may be our killer.

Before calling Morgan in for dinner, she continued with her analysis. "The girls were probably in the library talking about the dance. When was the last time you paid attention to the librarian in a library?"

I will from now on, I thought as she continued.

"The girls are seniors and a few weeks away from graduation, they don't care who knows about their plans. They talked loud enough for Monique to overhear their conversation if she was replacing books on shelves somewhere close. She knew they were planning to have vodka in the car, and that Caitlin was taking it from her parent's liquor cabinet. Monique had probably heard the same discussion before and just waited for Caitlin to make a mistake. She knew the kind of car Caitlin drives because she watches from her desk, through the windows that overlook the student parking lot." Sylvia winked at me, which meant she'd already been to the high school's library.

"Please go on," I said looking at my wife who was now pacing the kitchen, piecing the puzzle together.

"So my dear Holmes, the reason you didn't see Monique Fortier enter the school on the evening of the dance is because she never left. She had too much work to do and decided to stay. She planned to meet Emma later and help with the drink stand. From her view of the student parking lot she could see Caitlin's silver Cobalt SS pull into the lot, and then watched the girls cross the parking lot and enter the building. Then she went down to the dance, talked with a few of the parents, and posed for a picture or two. With her alibi established, she returned to the library and collected the vial of poison."

"Are you sure it was a vial?" I asked, teasing my bride's brilliance.

"My dear there is always a vial," Sylvia said, laughing a bit and then went on. "With the stolen keys and the vial of poison, she exited the building through an emergency door located in the library."

"What emergency door?" I asked, feeling stupid because all libraries have emergency exits.

"It's in the farthest corner from your conference room. It sits behind a tall bookshelf and it is easily missed."

She was being kind, and trying not to damage my already sensitive detective ego.

"It was dark. She walked across the parking lot and unlocked the car door. She has the stolen keys, so anyone watching would assume she has the same car as Caitlin, and wouldn't give her a second look. She poisoned the vodka, reentered the school, and made another alibi appearance at the dance, this time making sure that she appeared in at least one picture, and then on the security video."

With that said Sylvia turned to the door and called our daughter into dinner. My head was now spinning with a hundred questions that would have to wait until our family dinner was over.

After dinner Morgan went to her room, and I did the dishes while Sylvia read the newspaper. Once the dishwasher was started, I poured us both a small tumbler of scotch and sat down at the table. As she looked at me over her glasses, her smile said that she knew exactly how the pieces went together and that I had better be really nice or she wouldn't tell me.

"How did she exit the building without setting off the alarm?" I asked. "The doors are most certainly connected to an alarm system."

"Her accomplice, who had access to the school's security system shut off the alarm, and then turned it back on once the deed was done and she was safe inside the library," Sylvia explained returning to her paper while I pondered the possibilities of her theory.

"Alright, we can identify by virtue of the system itself who logged in and shutoff the alarms," I said. "The final question is why? Why did she kill Caitlin O'Brien? Monique had nothing good to say about Peters. In fact, had his death come by any other means, I would have looked at her first. Even if she still loved him and sought vengeance against Caitlin, why wait two years? She took immediate action against little Nathan Edmunds." I still didn't have a strong enough motive to explain Monique's actions.

"Why did Monique kill the first time?" Sylvia asked.

"Because she was in love with Peters and the boy threatened his career." As I said the words everything became crystal clear.

"I'm sure that you already know who her new love interest is," she said sipping her scotch.

Suddenly the look on Richard Baker's face said everything. His unexpected appearance after my discussion with Monique Fortier was a stupid, chauvinistic show of power for his new lover. She was threatened and he was going to take care of it. He is a very important man with lots of power and an uncontrollable hunger for the favors of beautiful women. Monique Fortier was just the next one in line.

"Why would she kill Caitlin O'Brien?" I asked.

"Let us assume that Caitlin knew about the affair between her mother and Richard Baker. If she did anything about it, she would be putting her own very comfortable lifestyle at risk. Based on what you have told me about the girl, she wasn't about to let that happen. Then she finds out that her mother's lover is also having an affair with Monique. Now she finally has her reason to take action against Baker. She was probably blackmailing him. Would you put it past her?" Sylvia asked with cool reason in her voice.

Then she went on. "From what you have told me, Caitlin was a very bad girl, most likely a sociopath. She never knew fear, and had never suffered the consequences of her cruelty. I'm sure she enjoyed tormenting Baker with such damning information. In his own twisted way, Baker is an excellent judge of the human psyche. He isn't stupid and easily picked up on Monique's emotional instability. He simply manipulated her, and then made her as the vehicle of his revenge. She was in love; she'd killed before and saw no issue with the removal of another troublesome child. It sounds to me like we have a killer, her accomplice, means, motive and opportunity." With the mystery solved my beautiful wife smiled in celebration of the victory.

"You are amazing," I said in awe of my wife's methodical reasoning, "and I promise you will be rewarded appropriately."

"Oh I hope so," she said sarcastically, blowing off my verbal advances.

"I need to prove that she put the poison in the lemonade," I said looking at the table and going over everything I knew about the dance in my mind. "They must know I'm close. Tell Morgan that she has to stay close to home. Unfortunately you'll have to drive her back and forth to school until this thing is over."

Suddenly what I said hit home, and Sylvia's look of concern turned to one of fear. There had been plenty of other cases and plenty of other bad people in the past, but never one with the potential to hit so close to home. "I know she won't be happy about it."

"Too bad," Sylvia said and instinctively got up from the table. I was sure she was headed upstairs to check on our youngest daughter. She would call Julia shortly and tell her that she needed to take extra care. I took her hand as she passed and rose from my seat.

"Thanks for everything and I love you," I said looking into the eyes of the woman that I loved more than anyone else.

"I love you too," she said and we hugged each other longer than we normally do, thankful that our marriage was strong and our family safe.

CHAPTER TWENTY FOUR

THE BURGLAR

On Friday morning, I sat low in my seat trying to avoid notice and watched a very brave woman directing traffic in the high school's student parking lot. It seemed that every student who could drive had a car and was now rushing to find the last available spots. From my vantage point I could see the wide, shaded windows of the school's library. I thought about my discussion with Silvia and the methodical way she explained the killer's actions.

From her desk, Monique Fortier had a clear view of the student parking lot. She would know exactly when Caitlin arrived that night. I could see the emergency doors on the side of the building, and the bright exterior lights that would have cast that corner of the building and the doors in shadow, allowing Monique to exit and then re-enter the building unnoticed. The double emergency doors lacked exterior handles and would have been propped open to permit her access back into the building, which further supported Silvia's assertion that she did not act alone. Someone turned off the alarm and then reset it once Monique had completed her task.

I saw Brooke Kincaid crossing the parking lot and I dialed her cell phone. I watched her fumble through her purse and on the fourth ring I heard her say, "Hello."

"Hi Brooke, this is Mr. Clancy, I'm in the blue Subaru to your right." Of course she looked left. "Your other right dear," I smiled and nodded to get her attention, "I need to ask you one more question."

She walked to the driver's side of the car. I didn't get out. After my confrontation with Principal Baker, I thought it best to remain discreetly out of sight, lest school security remove me from the premises.

"Good Morning," I said smiling.

"Morning," she said, and I could tell that she was noticeably embarrassed.

"Brooke, where did Caitlin park her car on the night of the dance?"

"We parked over there near the fence." She pointed to a row of cars; very nice cars that were backed into the spots along a fence that enclosed the track and football field. "Caitlin really liked her new car and didn't want anyone to door-dent it."

"Thanks," I said looking from the spot where Brooke pointed back to the library windows where I knew the Reference Desk sat. Monique would have had a clear view of the Silver Cobalt when the girls arrived.

"You're welcome," she said and turned to follow the students from the parking lot into the building. I watched her walk away. Within days her high school career would be over, and she would be headed to Hillsdale College, and a much deserved athletic scholarship. Brooke was a good student and an all-state long distance runner.

As the final students found parking spots, the morning bell rang and I watched a number of young men and women jogging to the school with backpacks in hand. The frazzled attendant made a quick pass through the parking lot. When our eyes met I opened the car door and stepped out.

"Good Morning," I said walking toward her, "just making sure my daughter found her way to school this morning. She has a bad case of senioritis."

"Did she?" the woman asked.

"Yes, and to sweeten the pot, I think she saw me checking up on her. Of course she didn't acknowledge my presence, but I think I sent a very clear message that should secure her attendance through the balance of the year. I also wanted to ask if you worked the dance last Saturday night."

"Yes, did something happen?" she asked.

"My daughter's car got scratched up and I'm hoping you might have seen something? Or perhaps caught some kids in the parking lot that didn't belong?"

It wasn't a good lie, but it was enough, and I watched her pulled a small notebook from the inside pocket of her jacket. Leafing through the pages she stopped and a wry smile spread across her face. "We did catch a couple of kids on the verge of doing something their parents would have been disappointed and embarrassed to find out about. Boy's name is Thomas Richardson; our Prom King and Football Hero. He might have seen something," she said closing her book.

"Thank you, I'll follow up with Mr. Richardson."

"You may want to check with the school," she said and pointed to cameras mounted on the exterior wall of the building. "If there was anything going on that night, the security system would have captured it." Then without another word she turned and continued on her appointed rounds.

I called Tommy's mother, an old friend and acquaintance. She picked up on the second ring. "Hi Andrea this is Gilbert Clancy." Andrea and I dated during a brief break-up with Silvia in high school.

"Hello Gilbert, what a nice surprise. How are you?" she asked in pleasant voice.

"Andrea, I'm investigating the death of Caitlin O'Brien. I was hoping to talk with your son." Suddenly the line went silent. "He's not a suspect. I think he might have seen something in the parking lot that night."

"Alright Gilbert," she said with a sigh of relief, "you scared me a little. As you know Tommy dated Caitlin for a few months, during what I hoped was a permanent breakup with Becky." I noticed the tone of distaste in her voice when she mentioned Becky's name. Most mothers feel that no girl is good enough for their baby boy.

"I'll send him a text message. I'll have him call you at the end of first period in about forty five minutes," Andrea said.

"Thank you," I said and broke the connection before I was drawn into a long and memorable discussion about our high school days.

My next call went to an old friend. "Hello," the man's pleasant sounding voice was barely audible over the sound of Bach's *A Minuet in G.* "Hold on."

I heard him lower the volume to a normal listening level.

"Hello."

"John, this is Gilbert Clancy."

"Gilbert, what do I owe the honor of this call?"

I'd come up against the Master Burglar when in a moment of weakness, that bordered on stupidity he decided to burglar The Guild. I think he did it for bragging rights, but as you can imagine Sal Bertini saw things a bit differently.

John was very good, he left no sign of entry and he tripped no alarms. The problem was that he decided to take a priceless bronze sculpture from Sal's desk. When I found him, Sal's team was closing in, so I convinced him that it would be to his best interest to give it back. I returned the piece to its rightful owner, who did not force me to reveal the name of the thief. The Master Burglar escaped a terrible beating or worse, and I gained an interesting business associate and friend.

"John I need a favor. Do you have time for coffee?" I asked.

"Of course Gilbert, and if I'm not mistaken there is still a rather large marker on the table," he said in a strong British accent.

"Excellent I'll be right up, I'm outside your condo."

The architectural tide had turned and Brownstone design was once again popular. John lived in a richly designed, multi-story condominium. I stepped to the front door and was greeted with an extended hand and a wide smile.

"Gilbert, come in."

I stepped into a dark paneled entrance hall. Before me a winding staircase climbed two stories, ending in what John called his music conservatory. From above I could hear Mozart's "The Marriage of Figaro." We walked into the kitchen with its Tuscan design and stone countertops. He handed me a cup of coffee, poured a second for himself, and I followed the Master Burglar into an octagon breakfast nook that overlooked a protected wilderness area.

"OK, what are you up to?" John asked as we sat down.

The man before me was about forty five and his brown hair was just beginning to show gray at the temples. He was small in stature, as most burglars are, and he was a very nice man, except for the fact that he stole from people to make a living.

"I've been asked to look into the death of Caitlin O'Brien," I said between sips of very good coffee.

"For a death that is most certainly a murder, I am very surprised at what little attention it has gotten. I was beginning to think someone was trying to sweep it under the carpet," John said looking at his bird feeder, where a violet colored Bluebird sat looking back at us.

"It's been quite a case, but I'm pretty sure I know who the murderess ..."

John cut me off. "They're the worse kind."

"Yes they are, and this particular murderess is a nasty piece of work. I know she did it. I know when and where, and thanks to Silvia I know the how and why."

"Then what do you need from me old friend?" he asked, getting up to refresh our coffee.

"I need your help placing her at the scene of the crime. I am certain that her image was captured on security video that resides in the high school. Having been banned from setting foot in the school ..."

"You would like me to remove the materials for you," the Master Burglar said finishing my sentence.

"Yes, and then I would like you to return them. They mustn't know that we," I paused, thought better of it, and corrected myself, "that you have taken them. When you return them to the school, I would like you to put them in a place that will be safe from people wishing to destroy them."

"I have an impenetrable vault in the basement," John said in a matter of fact tone, "they'd be safe enough there."

"Thank you, but the tapes must be returned before someone notices that the evidence has been tampered with. I am sure that the murderess and her accomplice have their suspicions, but I haven't pushed them hard enough to run." I explained the layout of the executive cul-de-sac and where I thought the tapes would be stored. John took notes and made a few sketches.

"I'll take care of it this evening, and drop them off at about ten thirty."

My phone rang. It was Tommy Richardson responding to his mother's text message. I used the call as a reason to excuse myself.

"Thanks," I said to the Master Burglar and let myself out the front door.

"Tommy good morning and thanks for calling. I spoke with the parking lot supervisor at the school. She mentioned that you arrived late to the dance on Saturday night."

"Yes, Becky wasn't quite ready when I got to her house," Tommy answered.

"Before going into the school did you see any teachers or members of the school staff in the parking lot?"

"Funny you should ask that, Becky and I saw Mrs. Fortier walking through the lot. She walked right past us, and by the time we got out the car, she was gone."

"Thanks Tommy."

"You're welcome Mr. Clancy." The connection broke and I walked back to my car. Silvia was right again.

When I got home Silvia had just returned from a walk with Mr. Jones.

"How far did you go?" I asked looking at the poor animal lying on the floor panting, after lapping at his water bowl.

She looked at me slightly taken aback, "Jonesy looked like he needed a walk." She took the leash off the dog and hung it on a hook in the pantry. When she returned to the kitchen she smiled. "By the way, the mystery hand at the dance belongs to a Ms. Rebecca Smith.

"Funny you should say that, because I just spoke to Tommy Richardson. He and Rebecca were both at the dance, and both saw Monique in the parking lot on Saturday night." Then I thought about the picture of the mystery hand, and those seated at the table. "Why do you think Becky was sitting at a table with the girl who stole her boyfriend away?"

"Hard to say," Silvia said as she knelt on the floor next to Mr. Jones, making sure he hadn't succumbed to too much exercise. "She may have been gloating that she had Tommy back. Boyfriends are just a game at that age anyway."

"Except for me of course," I said.

"Except for you my love," she said trying to not to damage my already fragile ego.

CHAPTER TWENTY FIVE

THE PARK

As directed by the Master Burglar, the outside lights were all off, and I sat in a dark kitchen, my mind running through everything that could go wrong this night. He was very good, but as I have proven many times in the past, even the best make mistakes. To my great relief a tap on the door signaled his arrival. At eleven thirty I rose from my seat, opened the back door, and found John standing in the shadows. Dressed in the black garb of his chosen profession, he was invisible against the night

"That was easy," I said, surprised that after our discussion only a few hours before, that John had completed his task and was now handing me the video tapes in a small black bag.

"Child's play, they really need to improve their security at the school. A real crook would have had a field day." He smiled and winked at the irony and comedy of his last statement.

"John, thank you. Would you like some coffee or perhaps something a bit stronger?" I asked hoping he would opt for the latter.

"How much stronger?" he asked smiling.

I motioned for him to follow me downstairs to my office. He

took a seat on the hand me down couch that had been a victim of Sylvia's latest decorating efforts upstairs and stretched out to relax. I opened a small cupboard above the bar, pulled out two glasses and my best scotch. From the small refrigerator; a memento of simpler times, I removed a small ice bucket and added a few cubes to my glass.

"You don't want ice do you?" I asked.

"Are you mad?" The Master Burglar said, appalled at the suggestion of such a violation. Sylvia preferred ice and soda with her scotch, which really sounded wimpy right now. Pushing that thought aside, I sat across from my old adversary and poured us both large tumblers, full of the amber colored liquid. We both sat quietly enjoying our scotch and I thought about who and what I'd become. Just days ago I was a Middle School Guidance Counselor, good at what I do and considered by some to be a professional. Now I was hiding in my basement, drinking scotch and accepting stolen goods from a man who should be in prison.

I raised my glass to the Master Burglar, toasted our good fortunes and we both took long pulls from our tumblers. I topped both off and then put the bottle away. There was still too much work to be done to be handicapped by a clouded mind.

"Two drink limit?" The Master Burglar asked.

"It isn't beer." I reminded him as I took my seat.

John raised his glass and smiled, "The nectar of life."

I smiled, nodded approvingly, and watched as he took another pull from his tumbler. I was sipping my own when my cell phone rang. I looked at John who was already getting up from his seat. I motioned him to stay. It was Bobby Thomas; I hoped this was purely a coincidence.

"Bobby."

"Gil, can you come down to the park," his voice sounded very serious.

"Sure, is something wrong?" I asked setting my tumbler down on the table. Sensing that I wouldn't be finishing it, John poured the balance into his own glass.

"Yes, something is terribly wrong. Monique Fortier has

committed suicide. There's a note with the body and she's confessed to the murder of Caitlin O'Brien."

"Alright, I'll be there in five minutes," I said as the connection broke. The Master Burglar was on his feet with a very concerned look on his otherwise cheery face. For the first time since I had told him that Sal's men were after him, the man looked scared. Perhaps he was losing his edge.

"That was Bobby Thomas. He just informed me that Monique Fortier has committed suicide. A note confessing to the murder was found with her body."

"How convenient," John said as he rinsed out his glass and set it upside down in the rack to dry. "You understand that I won't be joining you. The police of this fine village make me somewhat nervous. I'll stop by tomorrow evening and replace the borrowed tapes, somewhere far from harm's way." With that the Master Burglar ascended the stairs, departed from the back door of my house, and disappeared into the darkness.

I went upstairs and nudged Sylvia to let her know I would be going out for a while and that the alarm system would be set. She woke with a start.

"What's wrong?"

"Bobby just called, Monique Fortier is dead. I am going to meet him in the park. Apparently there was a note confessing to the murder. I'll turn the alarm on when I leave."

I grabbed my wallet and car keys. Sylvia got up, put on her robe and walked me to the door.

"Don't wait up. I will see you in a few hours." Sylvia hugged and kissed me. I pulled the door shut and heard the alarm activate. Baker had made a move to cover up his involvement in the murder. I still didn't know the exact reason why Caitlin was killed, and if Monique Fortier was our killer.

It took about five minutes for me to hurry through the village and reach the park, which sat on the bank of the Huron River. I arrived to flashing lights and an officer directing traffic. He leaned down to the car window as I pulled my identification out and handed it to him. "My name is Gilbert Clancy, Lieutenant Thomas asked me to meet him here." The officer stepped away from the car, made a call on his radio and then returned.

"The Detective is waiting Mr. Clancy." The officer pointed to an empty parking spot. When I stepped out the car I could see a group of police officers and fireman standing at the edge of the park's play field.

Monique Fortier lay just inside the woods. Both of her wrists had been cut and dark blood pooled in the grass. A hastily scribbled note lay at her side.

"This is how she was found," Bobby said drinking a cup of his favorite Starbucks coffee. "Ted, you about done, I would like to take a closer look at that note." He said to the forensic investigator.

"Yeah Bobby, all set."

"Thanks." Bobby reached down and picked up the note carefully. He read it and then handed it to me. I put on my cloth gloves and read it, careful not to touch the smudged fingerprints. The simple note said.

```
I killed Caitlin O'Brien. I cannot live with
myself or the guilt I feel. Emma, I love you
and I do not expect you to understand. I'm
sorry.
```

I looked at Bobby. He gave me a sarcastic smirk and a head shake that said exactly how I felt. This was all wrong. "Does he think we're that stupid?" I asked.

"Must," Bobby replied.

"She didn't come to the park, lay down on the edge of the play field, and casually cut both of her wrists. Women just don't do that."

"What do you think happened?" Bobby asked.

We stepped away from the scene, stood near a vacant picnic table, and I told him everything; the link between Peters and Monique, the possible source of the poison, and my suspicions about Richard Baker. I left out the video tapes. I would look at them when I got home, and John would return them later this evening.

"So now we have two murders and one suspect remaining," Bobby said. I could tell he was angry. "We'll have an officer stakeout Baker's house, and I'll talk with him later. Find out where he was this evening."

I went on to share Sylvia's theory about the affair that had most likely led to Caitlin's murder.

"We can certainly find out if either spouse is willing to report them away from home at odd times," Bobby said.

"Bobby, I'm really sorry. I wanted make sure I understood why, before I came forward with a formal accusation," I said, sickened by the thought that if I had acted sooner, Monique Fortier might still be alive.

"Gil it's alright. If you weren't pushing so hard, the girl's death may have gone unsolved." He patted my shoulder and then walked back over to join the other officers. As they placed Monique's body in a black coroner's bag, I turned back to my car. It was time to finish this thing.

CHAPTER TWENTY SIX

VIDEO TAPES AND LIES

When I returned from the park, I found the front door, back door, and the lights on the garage ablaze. Our normally dark yard was now brightly illuminated, a sure sign that my wife was getting nervous. Beyond the reach of the lights, the darkness remained peacefully quiet. I walked around the house and garage, not knowing for sure what I would do if I found someone hiding. Fortunately all was in order, so I turned off the alarm system and went inside.

I went downstairs, opened the black bag, and removed the three video tapes. Each tape represented a six hour period of the day on Saturday. Why Morgan and I hadn't thought to review them before was almost a grave oversight. I looked at the clock, it was three thirty so I opted for the tape covering the hours between 6:00 to 12:00 PM on the last day of Caitlin O'Brien's life.

At 6:00 PM the student parking lot was nearly empty, except for members of the track team just returning from a weekend invitational. Not long after the final student left, a black Buick Park Avenue pulled into a distant spot. The digital numbers at the lower edge of the screen indicated it was 7:30, which was confirmed by an orange sun falling quickly into dusk. Between 7:30 and 8:00 students began to arrive for the dance and the parking lot filled quickly.

I watched the attendant keeping order as she directed traffic. It was 8:20 when the Silver Cobalt SS driven by Caitlin O'Brien pulled in and parked at the very far end of the lot. After about five minutes of primping, Caitlin and Brooke finally emerged from the car. I watched Caitlin turn back toward the car and saw the headlights flash confirming that the vehicle was locked.

They crossed the parking lot and soon disappeared from view of the camera's lens. Almost undetected by the camera, I saw the interior lights of the Buick come on when the door was opened. Richard Baker exited the car and quickly disappeared in the darkness. The school's executive offices had a private entrance near the spot where Baker parked his car, and he would gain admittance to the building without detection. From the command center he would have access to the alarm's computer system where he could easily disable the library zone.

For almost an hour I watched the students come and go. At 9:15 Monique made her move. She crossed the parking lot with a quick and deliberate step. She either had nerves of steel, or truly felt nothing for the act she was about to commit. To the casual observer, she appeared to be hurrying to her vehicle to retrieve something forgotten. She walked directly to the silver Cobalt, the lights flashed as she unlocked the car with the stolen keys, and I watched her slip into the passenger side of the vehicle and close the door. I rewound the tape a second, third, and fourth time. Still, I could not see her activities once she'd gotten in the car. Two minutes later she got out of the car, locked it, and walked back to the school. The deed was done.

At 9:20 I saw the attendant driving her van through the parking lot. Her taillights flared as she stopped. True to her word, she got out and approached Tommy Richardson's car. A few minutes later, I saw Tommy and Becky walking arm in arm toward the school. As the van turned and disappeared from sight, I saw the headlights of the Park Avenue come on when the vehicle was started, and the bright-white reverse lights flared as the car backed out of its spot. With Monique safely inside the school, making her alibi appearance, Baker moved his car to the front, where he would make his own appearance. Things were quiet until 10:55 when the dance ended.

With the rush of students leaving the dance, I didn't see Caitlin and Brooke walk back to the car. At 11:00 the lights of Cobalt came on and the car pulled into the queue of cars lined up to leave. By 11:30 the final cars left the parking lot and things were quiet.

I looked at the gray light flooding in through the basement windows and realized it was six thirty Saturday morning. It was Senior Prom Saturday and soon our house would reach a state of mild chaos in preparation for the event. I would nap later and decided to go upstairs to make coffee. Sylvia was just coming down stairs with Mr. Jones in tow.

"Have you been up all night?"

"Yes, John dropped the tapes off last night, and you're right, Baker is behind the whole thing. At nine fifteen Monique poisoned the vodka, and then returned to the school where we saw her in the alibi photos. Right now she would be guilty of attempted murder, but how did the poison get in the lemonade?" I lowered my head until my forehead was resting on the heels of my hands. Sylvia set a cup of coffee on the table in front of me. "For sure the only murderer we have is Baker. He killed Monique to shut her up, confident that their plan to kill Caitlin was successful."

"I just can't understand why some people are so evil?" Sylvia said leaning against the kitchen counter. "What now?"

"We have all the proof we need to show that they are co-conspirators. Why did he park in the student parking lot? He could have parked in his reserved spot and entered the building through his private entrance. Instead, he chose to watch for Caitlin and make sure that she'd entered the building and wouldn't be coming out. Then he went to his office and turned off the alarm."

"How do you think they coordinated their plan? How did they communicate with each other?" Sylvia asked.

"Probably not with their cell phones, too easy to trace," I said, sipping my coffee and thinking of the possibilities.

"Email or perhaps they used instant messenger?" Sylvia suggested.

"Good guess, but probably not that technical. She probably just watched for him from the library window. They most likely ran through the scenario a few times. She was very cold and calculating, and she'd gotten away with it once before. I'm sure she knew how long it would take him to walk from his car to his office, and then to the alarm panel," I said, reconstructing my own version of the event. "I need to get into the school without Baker knowing about it."

"Why don't you just call Barti," Sylvia said suggesting the most obvious answer.

"Bartimus Brunt, the Dean of Students will most certainly have access to all security systems and keys to the building."

I looked at the clock, it was seven fifteen. "Too early," I asked looking at Sylvia.

"Not for this," she said and handed me the phone.

"Alright," I dialed the phone and it rang twice before Barti answered. I was relieved to find that I hadn't woke him up.

"Barti this is Gil, I need your help."

"Would this have anything to do with Caitlin's death?" He asked.

"Yes."

"What can I do?"

"I need to get into the high school. Can you have the school's IT coordinator meet us there as well?" I asked, hoping that I had his allegiance. He would be putting his career on the line if things turned sour.

"Baker is furious with you and Jim White. He says that your investigation has gotten out of hand. Of course I think he is a skirt-chasing idiot. When do you want us at the school?" Barti asked.

"Eight O'clock."

"Consider it done. Our IT officer is out of town this week, but I have someone who is just as familiar with the school's IT systems. I'll pick him up along the way. He won't be happy, but who cares."

The connection broke and an image of Betty McIntyre flashed in my mind. I smiled, shook my head and hung up the phone.

"You haven't slept yet, are you going to be alright?" Sylvia asked putting a pan on the stove and pulling eggs from the refrigerator.

"This thing has to end, and it has to end today," I said, and then felt my wife looking at me. She had a smile on her face that suggested I was getting a bit too big for my britches. She was right, these were tough words from the counselor turned detective.

"What are you going to do about the Prom?" Sylvia asked

Suddenly I remembered. Not only was it Prom night, I almost forgot we were chaperoning the event. Sylvia had already picked up my tuxedo from the cleaners, and bought a new dress that I wasn't allowed to see.

"I'll come home and get some rest. This is not going to mess up our family plans," I assured Sylvia as she handed me breakfast and then kissed my cheek.

"I love you," she said and stroked my unshaven face gently.

"I love you too."

"Keep Morgan close to home today. If she needs to go somewhere please go with her," I reminded my wife.

"I'll call Julia and tell her to take extra care today," Sylvia said reaching for the phone.

"I'm sorry about this," I said looking sincerely into my wife's beautiful green eyes.

"Gil, whether Caitlin O'Brien was good or bad, she didn't deserve to die. I know you, and I know you have to finish this. We'll be fine."

At seven forty five I picked up my car keys and cell phone. I looked at Sylvia and kissed her again in case I'd forgotten to and then headed for my rendezvous with Barti.

Chapter Twenty Seven

The Hacker

I waited in the parking lot of a strip mall, just down the street from the entrance of the high school. Barti pulled up in a new Cadillac DTS, a sleek black sedan with chrome wheels, and ebony leather interior. It appeared that being the Dean of Students was a very lucrative position. I was certain that Baker knew the type of cars that both Sylvia and I drove, and would be on the lookout for them. If he found Barti's car in the lot on a Saturday morning, it wouldn't raise suspicion.

"Barti thanks," I said slipping into the back seat of the Cadillac. Next to Barti sat a boy of about fifteen, he was bespectacled and his hair was messy. Apparently the boy had just gotten up, or perhaps Barti had just gotten him up.

"School's IT guy is up north golfing. Gilbert this is Jeremy Blake. Mr. Blake has a certain prowess with computers and IT systems; more to the point, he's the best hacker in the school. Jeremy has agreed to help us retrieve the required information in return for my pardon of his offenses." Barti smiled and winked at me. The boy said nothing, and chose to look straight ahead as we entered the long drive to the school.

I thought Jeremy's crimes against the school must be severe indeed, to get up and then without question join the Dean of Students on a very early Saturday morning mission. Morgan, who had remained out of trouble, or at least trouble I didn't know about would still be sleeping. We took a quick look around the school's massive campus and found it empty.

"What kind of car does Baker drive?" I asked wondering if he might own another car that could unexpectedly show up.

"A 2007 Park Avenue Ultra, black with chrome wheels, portholes, and charcoal-grey leather interior, very nice."

Barti knew his cars very well.

Satisfied that Baker was not around, Barti pulled the DTS behind the field house and out of sight from any cars passing through the campus. We crossed the parking lot and entered the school through the management offices. Once inside Barti turned to me, "Jeremy is at your disposal, where do we start?"

"First we need to see Monique Fortier's email account." Jeremy was already seated at Barti's desk typing commands into the computer.

"If Principal Baker comes in, turn off the monitor and hide under the desk," Barti said. Jeremy smiled back at him, knowing that his debt to the school was now paid in full. Barti closed the office door and left the lights turned off.

A few moments later the office door opened and Jeremy motioned us both back inside. When we entered, he turned the flat screen monitor around. "Was there something you were expecting to find?" Jeremy's question bordered on sarcasm and a harsh look from Barti extinguished his tone and attitude. Monique's email account was empty.

"Looks like Baker beat us too it," I said looking at Barti.

"Not quite," Jeremy said selecting the tab that said "*Sent.*" In his haste, it appeared that Principal Baker forgot to delete all of the messages. All the proof I needed was in a string of the last emails sent.

"We could have found it buried in the mail server if we didn't see it here," Jeremy said smiling back at Barti.

The last email Monique sent to Baker was at 9:26 PM on Saturday night. It consisted of one word, *Done.* "Jeremy, would you please copy the sent emails onto this." I handed him a portable flash drive and watched as he plugged it into the USB port in the back of the computer. I turned back to Barti. "We need to check the security system."

"I'm on it," Barti said pulling a ring of keys from his pocket. "Jeremy, when you're done with that would you please join me."

The young man looked at me with a plea for help. I smiled and then sat down in his vacated seat behind the computer. As Jeremy left Barti's office, he pulled the door closed behind him. I continued to look through Monique's email, looking up every few seconds at the entrance door expecting at any time to see Richard Baker.

The string of email also captured all of Baker's responses. As I read through the messages and responses that preceded Monique's final email, the conspiracy and the confession lay before me.

Baker 8:25 PM: *Her car is in the parking lot.*
Fortier 8:26 PM: *I see it. I'll go out at 9:15 and I should be no more than ten minutes. I need to get back to the dance and help Emma with concessions.*

I stopped a moment, not believing what I had just read. These two had carefully plotted to murder Caitlin O'Brien and she was still concerned about getting back to the concession stand. She was just as I had thought, cold and calculating.

Baker 8:26 PM: *You must be back in the building by 9:30 or the police will respond to the alarm.*

Fortier 8:27 PM: *I love you.*
Baker 8:28 PM: *I love you too.*

Reading the three most important words you can share with someone suddenly made my stomach turn. Baker was a master at manipulation and Monique was too weak to resist him. I looked up when Barti stepped back into the office.

"Gil, the alarm was disabled at 9:14 on Saturday and reactivated at 9:30. Baker used his own ID and password. Probably figured it would reset without incident," Barti said with a smile on his face. He knew what this meant. I looked over his shoulder and across the cul-de-sac of offices. Standing in a corner office, opposite Barti's, I could see Jeremy standing guard and keeping watch for Baker's arrival.

We walked back to the main security terminal. "I don't know why he did this," Barti said shaking his head, "the idiot could barely operate the system. The security company and the police were always calling me because he'd done something wrong." Barti printed off the security report and then locked the system with a new administrator ID and password. The system could not be accessed, nor could the memory be erased.

I returned to Barti's office, ready to hide under the desk myself, should Principal Baker enter the building. I was now convinced that we had our killers. I was certain that adding the cyanide poison to the vodka was done as a last line of defense, to ensure that Caitlin did not survive the night. I could place Monique at the dance, put her near the lemonade stand, and prove that she had access to a source of rhubarb for the poison. That was more than enough circumstantial evidence to infer conclusive guilt.

I thought of Monique Fortier, who had become a victim of the same crime she had been so intimately involved with, and would now escape prosecution. The other murderer lived, and very soon the proud and arrogant Principal Baker would be brought to bear for his crimes. Sylvia was right again, the character traits that should have identified the killers were right there in front of us all the time. Fortier was a hopeless romantic, insecure, and caught up in her own lovesick obsession. She was the kind of woman that a man like Baker preyed upon.

Caitlin O'Brien, knowing of the affair that took place between her mother and Baker tolerated it because of her mother's happiness. Upon learning of the affair between Baker and Fortier, she decided to use that information for her own benefit. What she hadn't factored in was the evil of Richard Baker, who cared only for himself and his own self preservation. Her childish attempts to blackmail her way into the School's Scholarship; a scholarship she never needed was the catalyst to her own demise. For Baker, removal of the troublesome girl was nothing more than a bump in the road.

"Gil, you alright," I looked up to see Barti standing in front of me with a worried look on his face. In his hand he held a CD and copy of the printout from the security system, which he would keep in his safe at home.

"Yes, we should get out of here before Baker shows up," I said as Jeremy stepped into the room.

Barti turned back to the now pardoned offender. "Jeremy, I want you to lock out Baker and Fortier's email accounts with a password of your own choosing. I don't want to know it."

"Yes sir," he said smiling and slid into the chair behind Barti's desk. I could tell by his enthusiasm that he enjoyed "sticking it to the man." I also handed Barti the security tapes from the black bag. He looked at them not to asking how I'd gotten them. Chances are they had come from his office.

"Please put these in a very secure place, they'll be needed later." I informed him. He shook his head and then slid them into his own brief case. A few minutes later we parted. I extended my hand to an old and new friend, thanking both of them for their assistance.

"Gil, let me know if you need anything else," Barti said and then drove away. I slid behind the wheel of my own car and called

Salvatore Bertini.

"Sal, sorry to call so early," I said as he answered his personal cell phone.

"Gilbert don't be silly, you can call anytime. What can I do for you?"

I went on to explain all that had transpired since we last spoke, and that I had all the evidence that I needed to take Baker down, and that I would need some help striking the final blow.

"Sergio and Armand are at your service. When and where do you need them?" As always Salvatore was a man of action and he helped me quickly develop the plan to apprehend Baker. It would take place at the Prom. With his only witness now dead and having confessed to the crime, Baker would consider himself beyond suspicion. I thanked Sal and broke the connection.

CHAPTER TWENTY EIGHT

MORGAN'S PROM

I woke at three thirty in the afternoon, feeling groggy and sore. I'd been up for thirty hours straight and a five hour nap didn't help much. I secretly celebrated that my latest assignment would soon be over and things would return to normal. Through the floor to ceiling windows in our bedroom I watched Armand's jet black Mercedes SUV as it pulled into the driveway. He got out, quickly surveyed the yard and the surrounding area, before rounding to the passenger side of the vehicle. I watched him execute the efficient moves of a well trained bodyguard. First, he removed Sylvia's bags from the back, and then he extracted Morgan, and then her mother from the still running vehicle.

The three disappeared from sight as they ascending the steps that carried them onto the porch. I heard the front door open and Sylvia enter the security code. At the sound Mr. Jones lifted a heavy head, thumped his tail against the floor, stretched, and then trotted off to meet the ladies. It should be noted that this does not occur when I come home.

In light of all that had happened, everything at my house felt normal. At the O'Brien house I was certain that things were much different. On an evening that should have been a pinnacle in the life of their beautiful young daughter, there would be feelings of overwhelming remorse and pain, loss and guilt. The home of Monique Fortier would be much the same. Through the actions of one very evil man, two families were shattered. My heart hurt for the Emmeline Fortier, who would now face this world alone.

I thought more about Emmeline Fortier and our interview, how much she despised Caitlin O'Brien, and then how she offered to help in any way she could. Did she know something then? At the time, I'd considered her a suspect and was wary of her actions. Could I have saved her mother from death if I had only stopped to listen? I didn't want to know the answer to that question.

What I did know of Monique Fortier was that her hand delivered the poison. She'd conspired with another person to take the life of an innocent child, and that she had committed that heinous act with great malice and no sense of guilt. Try as I may, I could not feel remorse for her death. As I have told my wife so many times in the wake of senseless murder. "They could have stopped, walked away, or simply said no." Monique Fortier did none of these.

The thought of a very pompous Richard Baker entered my mind. How could he do it? How could he go about his life with two murders weighing so heavily upon his shoulders? Then I considered the kind of man he was. Charismatic, charming, and a self centered womanizer. He was also the leader of the high school, the district's top job. That however, would end tonight. In a few short hours, the arrogant bastard would be escorted from the Baybrook Country Club in shackles. I was prepared to prove that he'd been the mastermind in the deaths of two women. I was drawn back to the present when I heard Sylvia and Morgan coming up the stairs.

"Hi dad," Morgan said looking in our bedroom door. She was smiling and looked beautiful. Her hair was up and her make-up perfect. She'd been transformed from my little girl into a gorgeous young woman. I watched her as she moved on to her room for more prepping. Her date for the evening was respectable young man named Alex, who would arrive at five thirty for pictures and the pre-prom festivities.

Sylvia closed the bedroom door, hung up her new clothes in an already too full walk-in closet, and lay down on the bed next to me.

"How are you feeling?" she asked.

"I'll be alright." Then trying to steer her away from any questions about Baker, I quickly added. "How was your day with Armand?"

"Armand," she said with a sigh, "is perfect." She collapsed, letting her body go limp on the bed. My wife is also an excellent actress.

"How so," I asked sarcastically, the game had begun and I would follow it through. My good friend Sal Bertini sent Armand to escort Sylvia and Morgan on their day out. Later, he would make sure that Principal Baker found his way to the prom.

"Armand is a perfect gentleman and extremely attentive to his charges." With those words, Sylvia looked at me and arched her eyebrows slightly for effect. "He stood by patiently while we shopped. He held our shopping bags and my purse. He dropped us off and picked us up at the door, and then he took us to lunch ..."

At that moment I would have sworn my wife swooned.

"And how was the spa?" As a treat Morgan, Sylvia, and Armand were treated to a few hours at the Amore Beauty Spa in Birmingham.

"Well," she said failing to hold back a giggle. "First, they had a very hard time finding a robe large enough for Armand. With that task complete, he enjoyed a few treatments, and then remained as always at our beckoned call. He took very good care of us."

"Very good care?" I asked teasing.

"Excellent care," she said and then melted back down onto the bed.

"What about the massage room?" I asked. The game of course had to be fully played out.

"Come to mention it, Armand decided not to have a massage. What would he do with his gun?" She broke out laughing. "There was a moment when a larger, stronger set of hands took over while

I was on the table. I didn't turn to look up, I didn't want to embarrass him," Sylvia said in a fit of the giggles. I hadn't heard her giggle like that in years.

"Armand actually picked out Morgan's hair style you know."

"Wow, he is perfect," I said, feeling very inadequate.

Sylvia got up from the bed and stood looking at me. "It is four o'clock and we need to get showered and prettied up by five thirty." She smiled at me and then pulled the bathroom door closed. Getting prettied up would be easy for my lovely wife. The world would just have to settle for me. I looked at the bathroom door and wondered how I'd gotten so lucky with her. I'll never know, but I am thankful every day.

At five fifteen I was dressed in my black tuxedo, adorned with a fancy green paisley vest and bow tie. Morgan nervously paced the living room waiting for Alex, not wanting to sit down and wrinkle her dress. She had grown up to be a fine young woman and I was very proud of her. In a week she would graduate from high school and then head off to Michigan State University to study Elementary Education.

At five twenty Alex pulled up in his dad's Cadillac CTS. It was a dark red and very nice. It was too nice for his seventeen year old son to be driving, but it was the Prom after all. He was noticeably nervous and dropped Morgan's corsage on his way to the front door.

"What a dork," Morgan said smiling as I opened the front door.

"Alex, come in," I held the door open and offered my hand.

He accepted it, smiled, and then he saw Morgan standing in the living room. He released my hand and stepped past me. "Morgan, you look beautiful," he said admiring her figure in the clingy gown.

"You bet I do," she said smiling and holding out her arm so he could place a beautiful corsage on it.

"Sylvia ..." I turned to the stairs and my wife was near the bottom. The red gown she wore was stunning. Having delivered two very large babies had not affected her figure, which was now accentuated by the evening gown. My wife was very beautiful. Fully done up with her hair curled and make-up, she'll take your breath away. I stared as she floated down the stairs with a lace shawl low about her shoulders.

"Wow," I said quietly as she stood next to me, and watched the kids.

"Hello Mrs. Clancy," Alex said looking up from the task of Morgan's corsage.

"Hello Alex, you look very handsome."

"Thank you." I noted the stutter in his words as his eyes took in Sylvia's beauty. I knew exactly how he felt.

"We should get to the pictures," I said lifting our Cannon digital camera from the table. I took pictures of Morgan and Alex, then Morgan and Sylvia. Alex took pictures of Morgan, Sylvia and me, and then finally from the tripod stand, one of all of us.

With the formalities out of the way Morgan left with Alex. He was a perfect gentleman as he opened the door and put Morgan into the passenger seat. She waved, we waved back, and then they were gone. They were on their way to pick up Morgan's best friend, Molly and her date.

Sylvia looked at me dabbing away tears from her eyes, trying not to smudge her make-up. "Well, our baby's gone and we won't have any more," she said her eyes were glistening.

"It's about time," I said turning towards the special cupboard in the kitchen. I poured each of us a small tumbler of scotch and handed one to her.

"Thanks for marrying me," I said toasting to more than two and a half decades of marriage. I drank my scotch and then turned to get another. The look of concern on my wife's face was unmistakable.

"Gil, you do plan on driving to the prom don't you?" She asked, sipping on her own.

"Actually my love, I do not. But he does." I pointed to the black Cadillac CTS-V sparkling in the driveway. Coming up the steps, Sergio stepped to the door in a tailored black tuxedo patterned red vest and matching bow tie.

Sylvia glided to the door and opened it. Sergio stepped in with a smile.

"Mrs. Clancy you look fabulous." Then he leaned down and kissed her gently on the cheek.

She blushed, "Thank you Sergio. I am surprised and pleased that you will be joining us this evening."

"Mr. Bertini asked me to tag along," Sergio replied accepting the tumbler of scotch I handed him. "Thank you, Mr. Clancy."

The phone rang and Sylvia stepped over to answer it.

It was then that I noticed a tiny microphone in Sergio's ear. "Excuse me Mr. Clancy," he said and also stepped away. I watched him quietly speak to no one in particular; the tiny voice activated Bluetooth microphone receiving and then transmitting his voice. A moment later he turned back to face me. "Principal Baker is on his way to the Country Club."

I overheard Sylvia say, "We'll want them in the meeting as well." Then she turned to me, phone in her extended hand. "Gil, would you like to speak with Bobby?"

I did, and then wondered why he had called to talk with Sylvia.

"Bobby, we are about to leave with Sergio. Armand has informed us that Baker is on the way."

"Okay Gil, my folks will be ready."

When I finished, Sergio and Sylvia were also ready. I closed the front door and turned to watch Sergio opened the rear passenger door, offer his hand, and then place Sylvia and her beautiful evening gown safely inside the car. He insisted that I ride in the backseat with my wife. As he closed the door I saw him say a few words, letting Armand know we were on our way.

CHAPTER TWENTY NINE

JUSTICE SERVED

The Baybrook Country Club is an exclusive symbol of the growth and prosperity that has found our village. With the rapid growth of fashionable subdivisions, fueled by the desire of those with substantial wealth seeking to be on the edge of the metropolitan sprawl, Milford, with its small town feel is a perfect option. These ultra wealthy would not be without the simple pleasures they had grown so accustomed to, and thus the creation of Baybrook.

Sergio's car passed under the arched gateway, and we followed a long and winding drive that rolled past a number of fairways, still full of golfers getting the most for their $50,000 per year memberships.

"This place is amazing," Sylvia commented as we drove past the front of the Venetian style clubhouse. At sixty-thousand square feet, the facility could meet the social needs that any of their members required. Tonight, it would be the Senior Prom. Sergio reached in the console and removed a VIP parking pass which he placed in the lower corner of his windshield. He glanced back at Sylvia, who sat in amazement and winked.

"Mr. Bertini is on the Board of Directors of the Country Club.

With that comes certain privilege. First, I will drop you off at the door."

Sylvia accepted this suggestion like she deserved it. I thought otherwise. "Sergio, there is no need for that," I feigned complaint, somewhat embarrassed to be chauffeured and then dropped off at the steps leading to the club's main ballroom.

"Mr. Bertini insists upon it. Mr. and Mrs. Clancy you have both done great service to this village that we so proudly call our home. Now, I must insist." Sergio had politely made his point and the discussion was over.

As we passed a gleaming black Mercedes, I saw Sergio nod to Armand, and then meet my eye in the rearview mirror. "Principal Baker has arrived safely to the event," he said and then queued up in the line of cars dropping off guests and dates. My stomach gave a lurch because we had now reached the point of no return. Had I done my very best? Had I truly left no stones unturned? My fear was eased with the confident touch of Sylvia's hand. She knew me better than I knew myself, and could sense the turmoil I was going through. I was about to accuse, and then I needed to prove how a well respected member of the community had plotted and killed two people.

We edged forward and I could see Baker's Park Avenue in one of the reserved spots. Beyond it, the parking lot was full of expensive Mercedes', Jaguars, and BMWs. This would be one of the rare occasions that Sergio's new Cadillac would not be the nicest, most exclusive car in the lot.

Sergio's car came to a stop, and before I could move he was out of the car, and opening Sylvia's door. I heard the soft rumble of the powerful car's exhaust as he offered his hand to my wife. She looked at me, smiled, and then accepted it. I felt like it was our own prom all over again with the addition of an exotic car and tall chauffeur.

Sylvia and Morgan had received some well deserved pampering today and I would always be grateful to Sergio, Armand, and Salvatore Bertini for the kindnesses and protection they had shown to my family on this special day. Baker's actions, based on what we had already seen were unpredictable. I got out, rounded the car and thanked Sergio, and then offered Sylvia my arm. I watched her take a deep calming breath, and we walked into the clubhouse to enjoy the biggest night of our daughter's life. A moment later Sergio appeared at our side, and together we ascended the final steps leading to the club's main ballroom.

Heavy wooden doors were opened by club attendants and we found ourselves in a large anteroom of dark paneled walls. There was a flurry of activity as friends met and others waited for dates. Having chaperoned a number of formal events at the school, we'd been given an earlier tour of the facility and knew where we would be seated. When we stepped through from the anteroom into the dimly lit main ballroom, the band was playing dinner music and muffled conversations could be heard all around.

Around the massive dance floor, fifty large tables were arranged in such a way as to allow waiters and waitresses room to move, and provide the guests easy access to the dance floor. This was the first Senior Prom at Baybrook, and the finest school event I had ever attended. I was brought back to the reality of the evening when Sergio leaned close and said quietly in my ear. "I will locate Principal Baker." I was reminded that while we were there to enjoy our daughter's prom, Sergio was there to complete an entirely different task.

The couples parted as Sergio politely made his way through the students. Conversations stopped and young ladies all but forgot their dates when he passed by. As he disappeared from sight, I sensed another presence by our side and turned to find Armand standing there.

"Armand," Sylvia said with a smile so warm and friendly, that I began to wonder if her stories from this afternoon may have carried some truth. I unconsciously looked to his large, muscular, and now manicured hands, and then just as quickly pushed a thought of the massage table from my mind.

"Good evening Mrs. Clancy, you look amazing." He was dressed in his own tailored tuxedo and just as much a gentleman as Sergio. I had to give Sal credit. He had two very fine young men working with him. Along with Sal, they had both become very dear friends of the family.

"Principal Baker is in the Ballroom," Armand said to me as we reached our table, which sat in a darkened corner and was lit by a few small tea candles. We sat outside the main activity of the prom, and we were soon joined by three other couples. The O'Briens, who were scheduled to join us, were of course absent, Sergio and Armand would occupy their seats at the table. Introductions were made and soon our attention was drawn to Richard Baker who rose from his seat and stepped up to a small podium.

After a short speech which celebrated the school year, he thanked the Prom Committee and the members of Baybrook as the prom officially began. The band began to play as waiters and waitresses delivered plates of food and pitchers of drink to the tables. In the clang of silverware and the murmur of discussion, someone tapped me on the shoulder. I turned to find Bobby dressed in waiter's tuxedo.

"Sir, may I have a moment," he asked.

"Yes of course." I placed my hand on Sylvia's arm, and she looked from me to Bobby. "I need to step away for a few minutes."

"Alright," she said, knowing that all too soon we would reach the moment of truth. Not knowing the waiter; both Sergio and Armand sat politely poised for action should I need an assist. I looked at both, nodded my head to assure them that I would be alright and they returned to their socializing.

I followed Bobby from the ballroom, across a wide hallway, and into one of the club's many conference rooms. He closed the door and I found two other men and a young woman whom I assumed to be police officers in the room already. We exchanged greetings and Bobby began. "In a few minutes we will inform Baker that some of the boys had a fight in the parking lot and security is holding them in this room. After he enters, he will not leave the facility, nor will he reenter the prom. Gil you did a great job. Your evidence is sound, and we have probable cause to arrest him and press charges. The plan is that you are to return to your table and watch for Baker to follow me away from his table. Once we have stepped into the hall, I would like you, Armand, and Sergio to join us. The two waiters and the waitress serving Baker's table are undercover police officers," Bobby said. "After Baker has been arrested, Natalie will collect Mrs. Baker and bring her to the conference room. Baker has shattered too many lives and we will not allow him to run or take flight." I was impressed at how Bobby had now taken charge of the evening.

I returned to the table, apologized to everyone, and finished dinner. While Sylvia and the others enjoyed animated discussion, laughter, and drinks, I watched Baker's table wondering when Bobby would make his move. As dessert was being served, a waiter, who was no doubt an undercover police officer, gave Baker the news. I could see by his expression that he was not happy about being disturbed. Being the tactful professional that he was, he excused himself and followed the waiter from the ballroom.

Sergio looked to me, rose from his seat and excused himself. Armand did the same, and I followed suit. To my surprise, Sylvia did the same.

"Please excuse us for just a moment," she said, and then we turned to followed Sergio and Armand from the ballroom. Baker was seated at the long conference table when we entered the room, his hardened confidence began to waver when our eyes met and he seemed to understand just how good I really could be. Sergio and Armand took their places at the exit doors, while Sylvia and I remained standing. Once every one was in place Bobby began.

"Richard Baker, very soon you will be placed under arrest for the murder of Monique Fortier and the attempted murder of Caitlin O'Brien." With a similar gesture, Baker and I both looked at Bobby. What did he mean attempted murder? I felt Sylvia's fingers wrap around my hand and she squeezed gently, was asking me to be patient. "In a moment you will be handcuffed and led out that door," he gestured to the door where Armand and Sergio stood, "and into an awaiting police car. When you reach the police station, you will be given the opportunity to call your attorney."

"This is preposterous. I had nothing to do with those terrible and unfortunate deaths." Baker's voice was strong and confident, even though his face was now ashen and sweat began to glisten above his lip and on his forehead.

"Principal Baker, you were directly involved in the planning and execution of both murders and we can prove it," I said and then turned to Sylvia, who on my queue began to unravel the web that Baker had spun so well. With her words, Baker's wall of defense began crumbling around him.

"Principal Baker, you have been in my bookstore any number of times and we know each other informally. You are beyond a doubt, what most would call a "ladies' man;" tall, handsome, charming, and a trusted pillar of this community. You also have a very keen understanding of the human psyche. Becoming the Principal of Milford High School meant you had reached the pinnacle of your career aspirations. Your many trips from Ohio to Michigan during that process put you in direct and close contact with Pam O'Brien, a very lovely and unhappy woman. You took advantage of her weaknesses and an affair ensued. I am certain that Pam was not your first extra-marital affair, nor would she be your last."

Baker interrupted her sternly. "What does that have to do with the current accusation?"

"I'm getting to that," Sylvia replied just as sternly, her eyes icy cold as she looked into the face of the murderer. "When the school year started, you met another vulnerable woman named Monique Fortier. Within days she fell deeply in love with you. She was so lovesick that it probably took you by surprise, but it didn't take long for you to gain control of her. You broke off the relationship with Pam O'Brien and left her broken hearted with a family in complete disarray. What you didn't count on was Caitlin. She knew of the affair and remained silent because her mother was very happy. Perhaps she thought that someday you two might marry. When you broke with her mother, Pam O'Brien was devastated. Typical for most girls her age, Caitlin let her anger and emotions override her common sense. She wanted you to pay for what you had done to her mother, and her thoughts turned to revenge. She was clever and decided she would destroy the one thing that meant more to you than anything else, your career. Caitlin was also very cruel. She could have simply gone to the district authorities with the story, but instead she wanted your pain and suffering to go on for as long as possible. She decided to blackmail you. First, she demanded that you fix her grades. Then you pulled the strings or made enough underlying threats that she was made a member of the National Honor Society. When she demanded the School's Scholarship, you'd reached your limit. How were you going to pull that off when there were so many more deserving students who should have it? When you told her that you couldn't or maybe that you wouldn't hand her the scholarship, she told you that soon all would be made public. You couldn't let that happen, could you Principal Baker?" Sylvia stopped for a moment. She was breathing hard and almost in tears as her own emotions were on the rise. Baker said nothing. Instead he simply looked at his hands, which were now crossed on the table in front of him. After gathering herself, Sylvia went on.

"Teachers began to question the favoritism that you were showing Caitlin. I can imagine that some may have thought the affair existed between the two of you. That would certainly explain why you made such a special case for a girl so openly defiant to the staff, one who had never delivered exceptional work, nor deserved a place in the National Honor Society. How did she do so well on her college entrance exams? Did you supply her with the answers or assign her a special coach?

All of this you did, because a silly seventeen year old girl threatened your professional reputation. You could have come clean, but what would that have cost you, your position at the school, respect of the community, and lastly your marriage?

As the school year was drawing to a close you had to do something. Any attempts to award the School's Scholarship to Caitlin O'Brien would have doubly blown up in your face. First, the scholarship would have been questioned and there would be an investigation, one you would not have survived. Second, there was Emmeline Fortier, the daughter of your current lover, a true scholar, and a well deserving finalist. You were entangled in the affair with Monique, and perhaps you had promised the scholarship to Monique's daughter instead. Your lies were beginning to close in on you like a noose; you needed to take action.

So you confessed your sins to Monique and told her about the affair with Pam. Then in a brilliant stroke you told her about Caitlin's blackmail, and how it threatened to ruin your career. Based on what Monique may or may not have told you about her past, you were pleased when she said that she would remove the problem. Was it you, or was it Monique that suggested the poison?

Monique had also risked a great deal in her own life. The affair was creating a strain on her family. She agreed to help you eliminate Caitlin, but she did so under one condition. You would divorce your wife and marry her. Of course you agreed, you were a drowning man, you would have agreed to any that would save you. With your short term problem solved, you were confident that you could manage the false promise that you had just made to Monique.

The library of a high school is neither private, nor is it quiet. Monique was the fly on the wall that no one notices. She heard the girls talking and learned of their pre and post dance plans. Having killed before, she began to make her own plans. She heard Caitlin brag openly more than once about the easy access she had to her parent's liquor cabinet. Monique knew that a bottle would be in the car on the night of the dance. She saw her chance and shared with you her plans to poison the girl. She also made the assurance that it could never be traced back to you.

So she stole Caitlin's car keys, and then from the library windows she watched Caitlin come and go. She knew the car and the spot where the girl always parked. She needed to secure an alibi, so she worked late and waited for Caitlin to arrive. But how could she exit and then reenter the school unseen? She would do so through the library emergency doors, which could only be opened when the security system is off. She knew that you have an ID and password to every system in the school, so she charged you with that task. What you forgot were the cameras that overlooked the parking lot."

Baker was now sweating and his skin was ashen. I could see him looking to the doors and windows of the room for a possible escape route as Bobby placed the security tape in the video player.

"This is your car," I said pointing to the Park Avenue and the prominent portholes on the fender. "You were waiting in the parking lot for the girls to arrive. Here is Caitlin and Brooke arriving and parking the car." Bobby advanced the video. "And here is Monique." The video showed her walking across the parking lot. A moment later the headlights flashed and she got into Caitlin's silver Cobalt.

"That's not Monique," Baker argued.

To squelch his momentary defense, Bobby reached into a manila folder and pulled from it an enhanced picture of Monique. In her hands she carried the latex gloves she would later use to cover up her identity.

"I also have two eye witnesses who will testify that they saw her walking to the car," I said standing across the table from Baker. "You became a murderer when you turned off the alarm system, allowing Monique to exit and reenter the building undetected. You may not have created, nor delivered the poison, but you provided the opportunity. And tell me this Principal Baker, what would have happened if Brooke or others had decided to partake in the vodka that night, mass murder?"

"That's ridiculous I stayed in my car to watch for students drinking in the parking lot. After most had entered the dance, I returned to my office to complete some work that needed to be done." Baker argued back, confident that he had found a loophole in our story.

"It was then, that you conspired with Monique by turning off the alarm system," Sylvia replied, pushing hard to break Baker's confidence.

"I most certainly did not. If Monique Fortier committed any crime, she acted alone," Baker said in a desperate plea.

I slid a copy of the security system printout in front of him with his ID and password highlighted, along with the times the system had recorded it.

"Someone must have used my ID and password," Baker argued.

On cue, Bartimus Brunt stepped into the conference room. "Richard, there is only one terminal to control the security system and it sits between our offices. The main doors from the school to our offices remain locked and under control by the security system. You entered and exited the building through our private door which requires a pass card and numeric sequence. This has been the security policy for years."

"Thank you Barti," Sylvia said and then she returned to Baker. "Maybe for the first time you saw the true nature of Monique Fortier and you were scared. You had just seen the way she disposed of the girl, and you knew you would never leave your wife, which now put every member of your family in danger. Any of them could fall victim to Monique's wrath. You had wandered into a very "fatal attraction" if you will excuse the cliché. Fortier was a cold-blooded killer, and a psychopath who felt no guilt and no remorse about killing.

Yes Principal Baker, your womanizing had come back to haunt you. You would never be able to protect your family, and never separate yourself from Caitlin's death as long as Monique was alive, and this is where we make our distinction between murder and attempted murder." Sylvia looked at me and then went on. "Up to this point Principal Baker, you were party to attempted murder; Caitlin O'Brien never drank the poisoned vodka. The poison that killed her was delivered at the dance, inside the school. Now that I have made that clear, let me return to my summary of events.

As I mentioned earlier, believing that Caitlin died from your plan, you could never separate yourself from the murder as long as Monique lived. So you decided that you would have to get your own hands dirty, and you set up a final rendezvous at the park." Sylvia stopped for a moment and drank from the water that I had brought for her. Baker still sat upright in his chair, listening to every detail. He was a strong man. Most men I knew would have crumbled by now.

"Monique had one weakness, and that was her physical size.

179

She was small. You easily overpowered and smothered her into unconsciousness. Not death, but unconsciousness, because your plans required that her heart must still be beating. Then you cut both of her wrists to make it look like suicide. It was dark and you placed her body at the edge of the field. With her you left the note, which was a very poor forgery. We have already proven that it was written in your hand." At that point Sylvia stopped her summary of the events leading up to our presence in the conference room. She was noticeably upset and returned to her seat next to mine.

After a moment of silence Baker finally broke down.

"I should have challenged her, and I should have let her go public. It would have been my word against hers, and with her reputation, I would have won," Baker said, looking at his crossed hands on the table. "Things became complicated. I was under an academic investigation and everything began to collapse." Then he said no more. Undercover police officers placed Baker in handcuffs and led him from the room. He was be taken directly to an unmarked police car and quietly ushered away.

When the door closed, I turned to Bobby. "What about Caitlin O'Brien?"

Sylvia rose from her seat and looked at Bobby. "Would you please ask Officer McCain to bring in our other guests?"

Bobby gave the order and Sylvia turned back to me. "We just figured this out a few hours ago. Sorry I couldn't fill you in, with all the prom preparations and everything."

"I understand," I said and took my seat at the table as Tommy Richardson and Rebecca Smith entered the conference room.

"Tommy and Becky please sit down." Sylvia gestured to chairs along the mahogany conference table. As both took their seats, I watched Tommy scan the room and all that were in it, much the same he did an opposing defensive line. I looked to Sylvia as she took a calming breath and began.

"As you both know, two weeks have passed since the murder of Caitlin O'Brien. The word murder is a very harsh thing to say, but there is no other way to describe her death. Someone planned, and then carried out with great malice, the actions necessary to end her life. I understand she was no angel, and I know that she hurt a lot of people, but she didn't deserve to die. With that said, I would first like to thank you both. Your eyewitness account of Monique Fortier helped bring a murderer to justice."

Both brightened and smiled.

"However, we have still not identified and brought to justice the actual killer of Caitlin O'Brien," Sylvia said.

I watched the relaxed look slip from Becky's face, replaced by one of confusion, bordering on fear.

"Mrs. Clancy, I thought you said the killer was caught?" Tommy asked.

"I did. Unfortunately there were two murders and two murderers mixed up in this ugly affair. One killer has been caught and the other is still at large, but I think you can also help us resolve that." Sylvia looked to Bobby, who handed her a manila folder, which she placed on the table and opened. From it she produced a picture that she showed to Tommy and Becky.

"Do you recognize these girls?" Sylvia asked. The picture she held in her hand was taken at the dance and showed Brooke and Caitlin, heads together with big smiles on their faces.

"Yes," Tommy answered right away.

"Yes," Becky said with a softer voice and a bit of apprehension. I noticed that she shifted her hands slightly. I turned back to the picture and the hand holding the napkin wrapped lemonade cup.

"I would like to direct your attention to the lower corner of the picture and the hand holding the cup of lemonade," Sylvia said and then pulled another photo from the folder. This time it was a blowup of the hand holding the lemonade and specifically the Milford High School class ring.

"Becky, this is your class ring isn't it?" Sylvia asked.

"Yes it is," Becky's voice was quiet and her face was growing pale.

Tommy looked at Becky in surprise.

I caught Sylvia's eye, smiled, and encourage her to go on.

"You were at the table with Caitlin and Brooke weren't you?"

Becky didn't respond. Like Baker she refused to meet Sylvia's eye, and choose instead to look down at her hands.

"That's alright dear; Brooke has already confirmed that you were there."

I looked at my wife glad I was not Becky, because Sylvia was all business. Like many people, her eyes are the window to her soul. Those eyes were now cold, reflecting the anger and disgust she felt over such a senseless death, and the motive for Becky's actions.

"Becky this is your ring. You are the only one in the school, in fact the only one in the history of this high school to order a ring with this Caduceus symbol." Sylvia pointed to the symbol on the side of the ring that looked like a short winged herald's staff intertwined by two snakes, accepted and understood symbol for medicine, and a most unique addition to a class ring. "It's my understanding that you are headed to Nursing School this fall. I also know that you work as a student volunteer in the Emergency Room of the Huron Glen Hospital." Sylvia stopped for a moment to drink from her water.

Tommy Richards was not the sharpest student in the school, but he knew where the discussion was headed, and by the look in his eye, he didn't like it.

"You've seen the effects of household poisons on patients in the Emergency Room," Sylvia said looking at Becky. "We were quite amazed at the simple combination of poisons that the killer chose. Then again it was brilliant, rhubarb for example can be found in half the yards in this village."

When Sylvia mentioned the rhubarb, I saw the muscles in Becky's face tense a little. I also watched her try to blink away tears. Sylvia had just delivered the gotcha.

"What exactly are you saying Mrs. Clancy?" Tommy asked coming to Becky's defense.

Ignoring Tommy's chivalry, Sylvia focused her attention on Becky. "Caitlin ruined your senior year when she stole your boyfriend, the Captain of the Football Team and the Homecoming King. It was to be your shining moment, and you were humiliated in front of the entire school." To my surprise Becky met and held Sylvia's eye. Neither broke their stare as Sylvia went on.

"You know all about common forms of household poisons. All Emergency Room nurses are trained to read the symptoms. You were surprised by the slow acting, yet lethal effects of the rhubarb plant. I found out after a little research that the leaves are the most poisonous part of the plant. Caitlin O'Brien as you know died from rhubarb poisoning.

Becky, you are the one who poisoned Caitlin O'Brien. You switched lemonade cups with her at the table. Maybe you only meant to make her sick, but the dose of rhubarb leaf extract was too potent. I would have thought it an accident, but when you added the Isopropanol your intent was clear. You meant to kill Caitlin and have your revenge."

I watched Sylvia destroy the girl at the table. Her facts were perfect and her voice remained calm and direct.

"You can't prove that!" Becky snapped back in her own defense. I looked at her and realized that she was at the end of her senior year and the end of her rope. She was eighteen and now a legal adult. The law and further proceedings would treat her that way.

"On that point my dear you're wrong. I was walking my dog earlier in the week and he pulled free while chasing a squirrel. He ran into your family's yard and through the rhubarb plants in your mother's garden. When I finally caught him, he had leaves from the plant tangled in his collar. I gave those leaves to Lieutenant Thomas, who submitted them for a DNA analysis and comparison against the extract that poisoned Caitlin. I am quite sure when the results come back they'll be a match. Becky we understand your motive, you had the means, and the dance provided you with the opportunity to kill Caitlin Keely O'Brien."

Bobby stood and took charge of the room as Sylvia turned toward me. "I need to get back out there before Morgan begins to worry." With Sergio at her side, Sylvia left the conference room.

After confirming with Bobby that he had all he needed, I left him and his team to deal with a hysterical Becky Smith, and rejoined Sylvia, Sergio, and Armand at the table.

"Is it over?" Sylvia asked taking my hand as I sat down.

"Yes." I was satisfied that with the arrest of Richard Baker and

Becky Smith that justice had been served. "You were brilliant in there," I said smiling at the only woman that I would ever love.

"Thank you," she said and pointed to the dance floor. I could see Morgan and Alex moving among the couples. She was happy and my life was once again back in order. Armand rose from the table and bid us a good evening. Sylvia stood, took his hand and then kissed him softly on the cheek. He smiled, held her eye for a moment, and then faded into the dark of the room. Sergio, who would stay and see us safely home tonight, had become something of a celebrity at the prom and many of the young women waited their turn for the next slow dance. All-in-all it had been a successful evening.

CHAPTER THIRTY

BACK TO MY DAY JOB

On Monday morning my office was quiet, and just the way I'd left it. The work that I thought would have been done by another of the already overworked counselors lay in a pile on my desk. My role as a brilliant super sleuth was only a side gig. My job as a counselor actually paid the bills.

I pulled up the dusty horizontal blinds and for a while watched the buses come and go as they completed their morning rounds. I glanced at the clock, it was eight fifteen. At eight thirty five I had my first appointment of the morning with a young man who would require some additional summer schooling. If that didn't happen he would be back with us in September to repeat the eighth grade; nothing like easing back into it.

Upon learning of my eminent return, Phyllis had taken it upon herself to schedule out my final days so that I would complete all my tasks in time. I pulled Dillon Hardy's file from the stack that coincided with my appointments and began scanning his records. His attendance had been extremely poor and his grades averaged a "D." I was beginning to have my doubts as to whether summer school would be enough.

Unfortunately some of the teachers in our school, already overworked are faced with a very difficult decision in cases like Mr. Hardy. Do that which is right, or that which is easy? The easy thing would be to pass Mr. Hardy onto the high school and let them deal with him. I'd already made up my mind that Dillon would not be one that we allowed to slip through the cracks.

"Good Morning."

I looked up to find my old friend Gabriel Osborne leaning against the door jamb.

"Gabe, come on in. I have a few minutes before Mr. Hardy arrives."

"Mr. Dillon Hardy?" Gabriel asked.

"Yes."

"Nice enough kid," Gabriel said with a shrug. "I just wanted to come in and congratulate you." He extended his hand. I stood and accepted it.

"Thanks," I said not hiding my smile of relief at having the O'Brien affair behind me. Gabriel and I had been lifelong friends, having attended school here, then in high school, and then onto Eastern Michigan together.

"I couldn't believe it was Baker," Gabe said in a muffled voice. "Who would have thought?"

"The thing was a tangled mess. Baker did a lot to cover himself. Actually, it was Sylvia who put it all together in the end," I said confiding in my friend.

"She is brilliant. Had you both not pursued it, he might have gotten away."

I looked at Gabe. From his statement, it was obvious that the whole story had not come out yet. "There were actually two murders ..." I was cut short by the appearance of Dillon Hardy and his mother standing in my doorway. I turned to Gabe, "Mr. Osborne we can continue our discussion in the teachers' lounge, say about three thirty," which meant we would retire to Tim's Red Dog for beer and popcorn.

"Alright," Gabe said and stepped aside to allow Dillon and his mother to enter my office.

"Good Morning, please have a seat," I said gesturing to my visitor's chairs. Gabe winked and left my office.

My meeting with Dillon and Mrs. Hardy was a minor success. After I calmed her down and she stopped shouting, we all agreed that her son was having some trouble making it to school and completing his homework. At the end of our meeting it was agreed that Dillon would attend the full summer school session, and go onto high school if he passed a thorough evaluation.

I was making notes on my discussion with the Hardys when Principal White stepped in, closed the door, and sat down. He was smiling and said, "Well, you did it again." For the second time this morning I was being congratulated for catching the bad guy. "Baker will be arraigned this morning for the murder of Monique Fortier, and the attempted murder of Caitlin O'Brien. There is no word yet on Becky Smith."

"Baker is going down. He was guilty as hell, and an arrogant bastard. He thought he could really get away with it. I don't know what happened to Becky Smith, she had Tommy back and her whole life ahead of her?" I shook my head, took of my glasses and wiped at my eyes. I was still tired from the weekend's marathon of activities.

"How did you get him, what was the final bit of proof?"

"Jim, what happened is that the girl was blackmailing him. She would have stolen the School's Scholarship just to take it from a more deserving student. She pushed Baker too far and he had to silence her. With that said, he should have been a man, stood up to his mistakes, and thrown her out of school. As his lies and deceptions began to tumble out of control, he reasoned that killing the girl was the best solution, so he conspired with Monique Fortier to kill Caitlin. Ironically, Becky Smith had also decided to take her vengeance against Caitlin on the same night. When the situation got out of control and the noose began to tighten, Baker decided to push the blame onto Monique, thus a murder made to look like suicide. Good or bad, Caitlin didn't deserve to die." That was all I had intended to share with Principal White about the actual case.

"To answer your first question, he made a lot of mistakes, and left a tremendous amount of evidence in his wake. I collected it, Sylvia pieced it all together, and now he will face justice."

"A job well done, please pass on my thanks and congratulations to your lovely wife."

"I will."

"What are your plans for the summer?" Principal White asked as he stood, prepared to get back to the business of running his middle school.

"This is a special summer. Sylvia and I are headed to England for a much deserved vacation, and then to Scotland to trace some family roots."

"Gilbert congratulations," Principal White said and offered his hand.

I accepted it. "Thank you Principal White." As I said this, my eyes were drawn to the door of my office and a very nervous girl who had come to learn the fate of her summer.

Purchase other Black Rose Writing titles at www.blackrosewriting.com/books
and use promo code PRINT to receive a 20% discount.

BLACK ROSE writing™

CPSIA information can be obtained
at www.ICGtesting.com
Printed in the USA
FFOW02n1358030215
10740FF